Darcy and Deception
A Pride and Prejudice Variation

Victoria Kincaid

ISBN: 978-0-9997333-7-0

Chapter One

"You must allow me to tell you how ardently I admire and love you."

Those words had haunted Elizabeth's dreams for a week. All of Mr. Darcy's words from that ill-fated night circled her mind like birds that refused to land, continuously intruding upon her thoughts. But the declaration of love, in particular, pushed itself into her consciousness again and again, a most unwelcome visitor.

Many of his other words that day had been painful and had provoked anger. Many she could dismiss as the result of his mistaken pride or his misapprehension of her character. But he had declared his love in an eloquent and heartfelt—and apparently unforgettable—manner. Those words could not easily be brushed aside or ignored.

The shock of Mr. Darcy's declaration had not worn off completely. At unrelated moments she would suddenly be struck with a recollection that the master of Pemberley had made her, Elizabeth Bennet, an offer of marriage. Even now as she watched the scenery of Kent stream past her carriage window, she struggled to reassure herself that the event had indeed occurred. It would be easier to comprehend the happening if she could speak with someone on the subject, but she had resolved to tell the story only to Jane. Nobody else would have the requisite discretion and understanding.

If she told her father, he would be incredulous before considering it to be the occasion for a good many jokes. Her mother would be in despair that Elizabeth had refused the offer. Kitty and Lydia would perforce share the news with the entire population of Hertfordshire—which was also true of her mother, come to think of it. Mary would moralize.

Only Jane will keep my confidence and will not laugh at my ignorance. Elizabeth willed the carriage to greater speed so that she might see her beloved sister all the sooner. She arranged herself more comfortably against the carriage's squabs and imagined the solace of Jane's presence. Her sister might also offer useful counsel.

Elizabeth could use some advice. Reading Mr. Darcy's letter had been a most unsettling experience. She had thought Mr. Darcy a villain and Mr. Wickham a victim, but the letter had revealed how wrong she had been. She had believed he disdained Jane's match with Mr. Bingley because of her dowry when he had believed her sister to be indifferent to the man. Likewise, Elizabeth had assumed he had observed her with disapproval and disdain when he had been viewing her with…longing.

Elizabeth closed her eyes briefly, still dismayed by the depth of her misapprehension. She still struggled to ascertain her own sentiments about the man. When Mr. Darcy had spoken in Hunsford, she had been horrified, but now…she knew that much of her dislike was based upon false information….

How did she feel about Mr. Darcy? Believing he held disdain for her, she had felt the same for him. But knowing he loved her…could she love him?

He was handsome, well spoken, and certainly eligible. They enjoyed lively conversations, and their tastes in books and music were surprisingly harmonious. But he was proud and difficult. Was he not?

If only she could see him with new eyes! More than once Elizabeth wished she could conjure him from the air so she might judge him with improved understanding. Perhaps she could have developed tender feelings for the man under other circumstances.

Elizabeth shook off this thought and gazed out of the window to distract herself, spying a stream and a patch of wildflowers that had just burst into bloom. How lovely. Yes, she would think upon these sights and ignore any thoughts about Mr. Darcy.

After all, her misjudgment of the man hardly signified. Their paths were not likely to cross again—at least in the near future. Perhaps in ten or fifteen years they might meet by accident when they were both married to other people.

Why did that thought make her sad?

***

"You wish me to go to Brighton?" Elizabeth could not believe she had heard her father correctly.

Her father nodded, regarding her solemnly from behind his desk.

In the fortnight since returning to Longbourn, her life had resumed its regular rhythms. Lydia and Kitty had greeted her with the news that Mary King had left Meryton, leaving Mr. Wickham once again available. Elizabeth had expressed no interest in the officer but had not confessed her complete change of heart to anyone in the family save Jane. It would be too difficult to explain.

She had twice been in company with Mr. Wickham, and she had managed to be civil while avoiding a solitary conversation. The news that the regiment would leave Meryton had relieved her greatly, but she greeted with alarm the news that Lydia was to accompany them to Brighton as a particular friend of Mrs. Forster's.

Now her father wished her to journey to Brighton as well? Although she enjoyed the seaside, her stomach clenched at this news. Elizabeth had no desire to chaperone Lydia or spend more time with Mr. Wickham.

When she had been called into her father's study, she had been surprised to find Colonel Forster occupying a chair. Colonel Forster's father was known to Mr. Bennet from his days at Oxford, and the two men had struck up a friendship over numerous games of chess during the regiment's sojourn in Meryton.

However, that did not explain why he was concerned with Elizabeth's visit to Brighton. She ventured the only possibility that had occurred to her: "You wish me to act as Lydia's chaperone?" Elizabeth could hardly decline such a request; her younger sister was dearly in need of guidance.

Her father leaned forward, clasping his hands before him on the desktop. "Yes, but that is not the main purpose for the request." He waved to the colonel. "Can you explain, sir?"

The officer shifted uneasily in his chair, cleared his throat, and then spoke slowly, measuring his words. "We have good reason to believe that George Wickham is an agent of Napoleon's."

Elizabeth gasped. "He is a French spy?" Mr. Darcy's letter had taught her that Mr. Wickham was not to be trusted, but she had not believed his heart was so black as to betray his country.

The colonel grimaced at her reaction. "I did not want to believe it at first, but the Home Office has intercepted correspondence that proves his complicity. Fortunately, he does not have the slightest idea we suspect him."

Her father interjected. "I had heard Wickham recently paid off large debts that he had incurred in Meryton, far in excess of what he earns as an officer."

The colonel nodded. "I, too, was curious about the source of such wealth. When a man from the Home Office approached me on the subject, I understood."

Elizabeth could scarcely comprehend the news. "That is treason!"

"Indeed." The colonel's voice was deep and ponderous. "We may only guess how much information he has shared with Napoleon, but hitherto he has not been in a position to do much damage."

Yes, Meryton was hardly a center of vital war activity.

"However," the colonel continued, "when we reach Brighton, he will be in position to collect far more sensitive information and quickly relay it to France. Smugglers along the coast traverse the Channel frequently with information—and a not insignificant number of escaped French prisoners. They have a bolt-hole near the town, probably a cave in the nearby cliffs. We would dearly like to know its location and the identities of the smugglers."

"Do you believe Mr. Wickham has been spying upon you?" her father asked the colonel.

The colonel nodded slowly. "Two letters we intercepted made reference to information Wickham should not have been privy to. It is possible that somehow he gained access to my private papers, or he may be working with someone higher in the army's command structure. In either case, we find ourselves in need of additional knowledge about the man's activities."

This seemed a worthy goal to Elizabeth, but why was the colonel telling her? "Why have you not arrested him?"

The colonel leaned back in his chair. "Wickham is at a low level in the organization; arresting him would not yield much information. The Home Office is hoping he will lead us to other agents and help us determine how he obtains such sensitive information."

Elizabeth still could not see why the colonel was sharing this news with her.

"Unfortunately," the colonel sighed, "I will have too many duties in Brighton to stay in Wickham's company and hope he might reveal some information. He is likely to guard his tongue around his fellow officers." His brow furrowed with concern; Wickham must be in a position to cause great damage.

Her father's eyes focused on Elizabeth. "The colonel approached me about whether Lydia would be willing to observe Wickham in Brighton and report what she learned."

Lydia? "Relying upon her would be a disaster!" Elizabeth exclaimed immediately. "She could not keep a secret if her life depended on it."

Her father's mouth curved in an ironic smile. "Just so. I told the colonel Lydia is too young and unreliable for such a weighty task. Yet it is vitally important. I did mention that Wickham had shown an interest in you, and the colonel inquired whether you would be amenable to such an assignment."

Good Lord! Such a great responsibility. She hardly knew if she was equal to such a task. Her skin prickled, and perspiration dripped down her back as she sat still under the scrutiny of the two men.

As if reading her mind, her father said, "I know you would perform such duties admirably."

Elizabeth welcomed the praise but wished that she could share her father's confidence. Everything she knew of espionage she had gleaned from novels, and most likely they did not enjoy a high degree of accuracy.

The colonel cleared this throat. "I assure you that Wickham will never learn of your involvement, and I would not ask you to undertake anything dangerous or disagreeable. You would merely keep company with him at Brighton's many balls, dinners, and card parties and observe him. He might reveal something about the source of his sensitive information, the identity of his co-conspirators, or the location of the spies' hideout. He is apt to speak more freely around a lady than he would with a fellow officer."

Naturally. No man would suspect a *woman* to concern herself with information about the war. Elizabeth experienced a hot rush of anger on behalf of her sex. *Perhaps we cannot be soldiers, but we are not altogether useless.*

"You could stay at my house with your sister and my wife. This would put you in position to relay any information to me," the colonel said. "It would also give you an opportunity to learn if he is intercepting my post or sneaking into my study when I am away."

Elizabeth was flattered by the trust the colonel exhibited in her discretion and judgment. However, it was such a weighty responsibility! The future of England could depend upon her actions. Her mind could scarcely grasp the enormity of the task.

Her father steepled his fingers. "The colonel and I have discussed this operation at some length. You will never be alone with Mr. Wickham, and you may beg the colonel's assistance if a difficult situation arises. Of course, you may also return home at any time." His eyes narrowed. "I would not risk your safety for anything in the world."

"I know, Papa." The comforting words nonetheless sent a chill through her. Her father must believe the threat to England was quite grave or he would not even consider such an undertaking.

As a woman, Elizabeth had never believed she would have an opportunity to serve her country. She could not deny a thrill at the idea of such an interesting and exciting task.

"I pray you do not experience a sense of obligation," the colonel said urgently. "You are but a woman, and a young one at that." Elizabeth's spine stiffened, and her hands clenched into fists. "If you are too frightened—"

Elizabeth interrupted. "I am not frightened."

A faint smile flashed across her father's face.

"I can be cautious enough to mitigate the danger, and I may be alert for useful information," she continued. "I am happy to accept your assignment."

The colonel leaned back in his chair with a relieved smile; obviously her acceptance had been of importance to him.

"But how should we explain my sudden desire to visit Brighton?"

"Ah, yes." Her father's proud smile fade into an expression of anxiety. "As you guessed, I might send you to Brighton as a sort of chaperone for Lydia—despite your objections, naturally."

Elizabeth grimaced. Under other circumstances she would object strenuously.

"My wife would be happy for the company of another lady," the colonel said, "and our house in Brighton will have sufficient space for another guest. You should be quite comfortable."

Her father watched her steadily. "I am sorry we must share such ill news about Mr. Wickham." Of course, he did not know that Mr. Darcy's letter had prepared her for thoughts of the officer's perfidy.

Still, Elizabeth suppressed a shudder at the sound of the man's name. Could she do it? Knowing his character as she did, could she allow him to court her? Dance with him? Converse freely with him? Perhaps kiss him? Yes, she had once thought him handsome, but knowing the blackness of his soul, could she pretend attraction to him?

Elizabeth squared her shoulders. She must do so. She must convince him that she cared for him. At any moment the tide of the war might turn against Britain. How could she continue with her life as usual knowing she might prevent such evil?

No, her duty was clear.

"Very well, Colonel Forster," she said. "Tell me what I need to know."

Chapter Two

Darcy beheld the door to the Hursts' house with great reluctance, staring at the ornate brass knocker as if it were a snake prepared to sink its fangs into his hand. The house itself was inoffensive, a respectable size and well-decorated, but the occupants...well, one occupant in particular.

Darcy ground his teeth. *I must speak with Bingley. I have no choice.* But the reminders did nothing to calm the queasy sensations in his stomach. *This is unavoidable.* That thought did not help either.

His conversation with Elizabeth at Hunsford Parsonage had elucidated several facts to Darcy, among them how wrong he had been about Jane Bennet's feelings for Bingley. Elizabeth's distress could only be a result of her sister's deep suffering. It was also true that Bingley had been mired in melancholy since leaving Netherfield. Darcy had a duty to both Miss Bennet and Bingley to reveal what he knew to his friend.

How would Bingley react to the news? He would be within his rights to challenge Darcy to a duel for meddling in his life. More likely, he would simply toss Darcy out of the house with a command never to darken the door again. Darcy would be unable to argue; he certainly deserved such treatment.

Nothing matters as long as I repair the damage I have done. If he repeated this frequently enough, he might start to believe it.

Hopefully he could enjoy a moment alone with Bingley. Miss Bingley and her sister, Mrs. Hurst, were liable to monopolize the conversation, and Darcy could scarcely discuss Jane Bennet in their presence. If only Bingley had his own townhouse in London. Instead, his friend had stayed at Darcy House until Darcy's departure for Rosings Park, and then he had repaired to the Hursts' house in Grosvenor Square. Bingley was a forbearing sort, but even his formidable patience must be wearing thin after a month here.

Enough dawdling. Darcy steeled his spine and banged the knocker sturdily three times.

By the time the footman had taken his coat and directed Darcy to a drawing room, he was convinced this was the worst idea he had ever conceived. But he was committed now.

Darcy did not have long to wait before Bingley bounced into the room, giving Darcy's hand a hearty shake. "Darcy! You are just what I need to liven up a dull day! Caroline and Louisa have gone shopping, and Hurst is off taking a nap somewhere."

Thank God.

Bingley sat and immediately leaned forward eagerly in his chair. "I have not seen you since your return from Kent—what, it must be nearly two weeks now!"

Darcy fiddled with his watch fob. "Yes, I apologize for not visiting earlier. Quite a bit of business had accumulated during my absence." Not incorrect, but it certainly did not reveal the whole story. In truth, Darcy had been dreading this conversation and taken a while to work up the courage.

Bingley waved away the apology. "No matter! No matter! Although you are a welcome sight. London has been rather dull while you were gone."

Darcy could only hope that Bingley was still as enthusiastic about their friendship in a half hour. *Best to get it over with.* He took a deep breath. "I have a confession to make."

"Oh?" One of Bingley's eyebrows rose, although his smile did not dim.

Darcy rubbed both hands over his face. "I…uh…in January, Miss Bennet…Miss Jane Bennet was here, visiting London for two months…and I…kept the information from you."

Bingley stiffened as if shock had paralyzed his muscles. "What? You kept the…?" He swallowed loudly. "How did you learn of her presence?" he asked slowly.

Darcy had known he would need to name his co-conspirators, and this had occasioned some misgivings. "Your sisters so informed me. They were concerned for your peace of mind."

Bingley's left hand was shaking where it grasped the arm of the chair. "And who are they to make such decisions for me? Who are you?" His voice was low and dangerous.

"I agree." Darcy blew out a breath. "It was wrong of us. We should not have concealed it."

Bingley leapt from his chair and commenced pacing with great energy. "It was *very* wrong of you!"

Darcy could do nothing but fall on his sword. Best to give all the bad news at once. "Yes. I also believe—I believe now that we were wrong in encouraging you to quit Hertfordshire."

Bingley paused and then whirled around to face Darcy. "You admit you were wrong?"

"Utterly and completely. You have my most abject apologies."

Bingley stared into the empty fireplace, pushing a shaky hand through his hair. "Why tell me now?"

With hands clenching the arms of his chair, Darcy could not prevent himself from gazing longingly at the exit. As bad as the previous conversation had been, the next part would be even worse. "I...encountered Miss Elizabeth Bennet at Rosings, and she...implied that your actions—the actions we encouraged you to take—had saddened her sister." No, that was not quite the truth, and Darcy intended to reveal the whole truth. "No, had...broken her sister's heart."

"Oh, Good Lord!" Bingley fell into a chair, burying his face in his hands.

"I cannot apologize enough. I truly believed it to be the right course at the time." It was a meager excuse. At the time he had believed his advice to Bingley to be objective and unbiased, but now he realized it had been colored by Darcy's own desire to escape his attraction to Elizabeth.

Bingley's head turned sharply in Darcy's direction. "Why did Miss Elizabeth reveal such personal information? That seems unlike her."

Darcy winced. He had hoped Bingley would not notice that little incongruity in his story—particularly since Darcy had promised himself he would not lie to his friend again. "I...um..." The words emerged slowly as if dragged from his throat. "She was very angry with me and accused me of ruining her sister's happiness."

Bingley frowned. "Why was she angry with you? What did you do to her?"

Darcy's honor was piqued. What did Bingley think he had done? He would not be offensive to Elizabeth! "I-I made her an offer."

Bingley's mouth fell open. "Of marriage?"

"Yes." Darcy would not meet his friend's eyes. He would see incredulity, but would he also see pity? That would almost be worse.

"After you declared that the Bennet family's connections were too common for me?"

"Yes."

"You understand my confusion." Bingley's voice had a dangerous edge.

"Of course, but…" How could he explain it when he barely understood it himself? "It was different…"

Bingley was on his feet again, looming over Darcy's chair. Suddenly the prospect of a duel did not seem impossible. "Oh? How was it different?" he asked in a low growl.

Damnation! Darcy hated revealing himself in this way! Such information should be private, but Bingley deserved the truth. "When I saw Elizabeth at Rosings, I realized I had…fallen in love with her, Charles. I could not imagine my life without her."

"Oh." Bingley's eyes widened, and he retreated several steps. "I-I see. Good…excellent." He swallowed. "Let me offer you my congratulations."

"There is no need." Darcy strove to keep the bitterness from his tone. "She refused me."

"She—what?" Bingley said. "Are you certain you heard her correctly?"

Darcy snorted. "There is nothing wrong with my hearing. She was quite insistent; there was no mistaking her meaning. She does not like or respect me—which, you must admit, are excellent reasons for refusing an offer."

Bingley blinked rapidly. "Huh. I knew she found you a little high-handed, but I did not realize… Well, I had no idea you were partial toward her, so I was oblivious to much."

"I took pains to conceal my sentiments."

Bingley nodded in an abstracted way. After a minute he asked, "Have you tried to change Miss Elizabeth's opinion of you?"

"No, I left Rosings the next day."

"I believe you would make a good match. You should—"

Darcy interrupted him, having no desire to revisit the frustration and melancholy Elizabeth's very name provoked. "I did not visit to discuss *my* affairs; I came to discuss yours," Darcy reminded him. "Given what we now know, I believe you should return to Hertfordshire and resume your courtship of Miss Bennet."

"Hmm…" Bingley tapped one finger against his mouth.

Why had his friend not already ordered his horse saddled? "It is not too late," he murmured softly. "I believe she is still unattached. If you still have feelings for her—"

"*If!*" Bingley said with a short laugh. "I only think of her half a dozen times a minute!"

"Then you should leave for Hertfordshire and declare yourself."

Bingley nodded slowly. "I will do so on one condition: that you accompany me on the trip and speak with Miss Elizabeth again."

The very thought filled Darcy with terror. "There is nothing left to say."

Bingley stood, clapping his friend on the shoulder. "I doubt that. She was angry over your highhandedness; it does not necessarily follow that she will hate you for the rest of her life."

"My standards for my betrothed are higher than the cessation of animosity," Darcy said with a grimace.

Bingley said nothing but stared out of the window. Darcy waited; his friend must go to Hertfordshire. Nothing else would lessen the damage wrought by his actions. Finally, Bingley lifted his chin. "You must come with me, or I will not go."

Darcy sighed; Hertfordshire was the last place on earth he wished to visit. The very thought caused his heart to race. But he owed his friend an enormous debt, and this would be his penance. "Very well. I will come. But do not be surprised if Miss Elizabeth refuses to speak with me."

***

The most notable feature of Longbourn's drawing room was the absence of one Elizabeth Bennet. Upon their arrival, Mrs. Bennet had risen and granted Bingley an effusive welcome while Jane Bennet granted him a shy smile that boded well for the man's future chances at matrimonial bliss. Two of the younger sisters were also present.

Mrs. Bennet's welcome to Darcy was far less enthusiastic; he might have been tempted to call it curt. Whatever other faults one might lay at her door, she was not prone to forgetfulness—particularly when it came to perceived slights. Darcy's fortune would not restrain her dislike of him. He grudgingly admired someone who adhered so closely to her "principles" despite the social and monetary advantages Darcy's friendship could convey.

Bingley sat beside Miss Bennet while Darcy chose a chair as far from Mrs. Bennet as possible, near the window and beside Mary Bennet, who barely peered up from her book of sermons long enough to acknowledge the visitors' arrival. He believed the other daughter was Kitty, which meant the youngest, Lydia, was absent along with Elizabeth.

After a few minutes of desultory conversation, Darcy's relief at not immediately encountering Elizabeth gave way to concern. Where was she? Was she lurking upstairs, having refused to see him? Was she ill? Darcy longed to inquire but feared any questions might draw attention to his interest in Elizabeth.

Of course, she and Lydia might be visiting friends or buying ribbons in Meryton. Taking a sip of tea, Darcy hoped to soothe his nervous stomach. There was absolutely no reason to fret. Her absence is a boon, he reminded himself, yet the lack of Elizabeth gnawed on his nerves.

The conversation had turned from the state of the roads to the unusual warmth of the weather. When Mrs. Bennet launched into a detailed description of her friends' various health complaints, Darcy allowed his attention to wander. His gaze frequently drifted to the window in the hopes of spying Elizabeth on the road.

"—since Lydia and Lizzy are away—"

"I beg your pardon?" Darcy said.

Mrs. Bennet blinked; Darcy *had* interrupted rather suddenly. "Where did you say El—your other daughters are at present?"

Mrs. Bennet sniffed. "I did not say, but they are gone to Brighton with Colonel Forster's regiment. Lydia is a particular friend of Mrs. Forster's—and such a favorite with all the officers!" she crowed. "And Lizzy has gone to keep her sister company," she added as an afterthought.

Recalling Miss Lydia's behavior, Darcy concluded that Elizabeth's purpose was to prevent her sister from shaming the family. Regardless, she was not at Longbourn.

Darcy set his teacup down on the saucer so forcefully it clanged, causing everyone to glance in his direction. *Devil take it!* Not only was Elizabeth gone, but she was at Brighton surrounded by hundreds of lonely soldiers. Of course, he had not expected anything of a romantic nature to occur, but he had thought to catch a glimpse of her.

Darcy grasped the arms of his chair, resisting the impulse to leap to his feet and demand a horse for Brighton at once. He had no reason for visiting the seaside resort, and Elizabeth would not be pleased to see him there.

Bingley's face held great sympathy. *I hope my distress is not so obvious to the others.*

Mrs. Bennet was still rattling on about Brighton. "Lizzy is not quite so popular with all the officers, but one of them has taken a fancy to her." She gave Darcy a meaningful glare. With a stab of panic, he realized she meant Wickham. But surely Elizabeth was immune from Wickham's charms after reading Darcy's letter at Hunsford.

Only now did Darcy realize how much he had wanted to see Elizabeth at Longbourn. Although he had tried to quell any hopes, he had still imagined conversations in which he sought her forgiveness and persuaded her to accept a courtship. Now the prospect of several days at Netherfield felt hollow and pointless.

"Darcy?" Bingley's voice shook him from his reverie.

"Hmm?"

"You were woolgathering." His friend chuckled.

Darcy scowled. He disliked laughter at his expense, particularly when he was already out of sorts.

"We are taking a walk, and I asked if you would join us," Bingley said.

An escape from Mrs. Bennet's prattle? "It would be my pleasure."

Apparently, Mary Bennet did not care for walks, so the party consisted of Miss Jane, Miss Catherine, Bingley, and Darcy. Remembering Kitty from his previous sojourn in Hertfordshire, Darcy fervently hoped that she remained fixated on red coats and had not acquired an interest in men of large fortune.

As the ladies donned light wraps in the front hallway, the younger Miss Bennet treated Darcy with such complete indifference that his fears were allayed. Within minutes the quartet was strolling along the dusty country road.

Jane and Bingley were immediately engrossed in earnest conversation, which apparently required a walking pace that a slug would find tedious. Kitty and Darcy soon left them far behind.

Darcy strode beside the younger Miss Bennet in silence. What could he possibly say to a girl of this age? All he knew of her was that she liked men in red coats—hardly an appropriate subject for conversation.

However, Kitty might have copious information on one topic of keen interest to Darcy and no doubt she would be indiscreet enough to share it. "I was surprised to learn that your sisters were gone to Brighton," he said.

Kitty kicked at a stone in the road. "Everything is so dull in Meryton now, and Lydia is enjoying herself in Brighton. It isn't fair! I am older; I should have been the one to go!"

Best to direct the conversation in other directions. "I was surprised that Miss Elizabeth accompanied her. Is she a particular friend of Mrs. Forster's as well?"

"She is not, to be sure!" Kitty's tone turned peevish. "Lizzy is scarcely acquainted with Mrs. Forster, but Papa insisted that she must go."

This lent credence to the idea that Elizabeth was to serve as a sort of chaperone for her younger sister, hardly an enviable position.

Kitty continued. "There is nothing for her in Brighton. Lizzy does not even care for the officers!" Relief surged through Darcy, but then she added, "Well, except for Mr. Wickham, of course."

Darcy nearly tripped over his own feet. "Wickham?"

Kitty's sidelong glance suggested she had heard much of Wickham's slander. "Yes, he is quite Lizzy's favorite."

Darcy was finding it difficult to breathe. "When I encountered her in Kent, I was of the impression that her friendship with Mr. Wickham had, er, waned," he managed to say.

Kitty squinted at him. "You saw Lizzy in Kent?"

Elizabeth had concealed his presence at Rosings? Why? He could understand avoiding the details of his disastrous marriage proposal, but was it necessary to hide their entire encounter?

"Er, yes. Mr. Collins is my aunt's parson." Darcy thought it best to give as little explanation as possible.

"Huh."

Darcy needed to learn more. "I thought Miss Elizabeth did not care for Mr. Wickham," he prompted.

Kitty shrugged. "She was vexed when he was courting Mary King, but that came to an end while Lizzy was away."

Surely Elizabeth would not have returned Wickham's interest after returning from Kent. When she read Darcy's letter… "Miss Elizabeth was still on good terms with Mr. Wickham?" Hearing the incredulity in his own voice, Darcy was not surprised at Kitty's searching look.

"Oh yes!" Kitty declared without hesitation. "It was as if Mary King had never existed and Lizzy had never left. I actually"—the girl lowered her voice and inclined her head toward Darcy's, although there was no one nearby to hear her secret—"spied them in the garden! They didn't even notice me." She giggled.

"Alone in the garden?" The mere image filled Darcy with horror.

"I even saw him"—she paused for dramatic effect—"kiss her!"

"K-Kiss?" Darcy could not breathe.

Kitty held a hand to her heart. "It was so romantic—just as it was described in *The Castle of Otranto*. Have you read it? It is terribly good!"

Darcy tried and failed rather spectacularly to avoid picturing Wickham kissing Elizabeth. It was all too easy to imagine. His chest ached from lack of air—or was that pain in his heart?

A sudden thought struck him. "Did he force her into it?"

Kitty's brows drew together. "Of course not. She was smiling."

Turning away from Kitty, Darcy concentrated on not being sick by the side of the road.

"He is frightfully handsome, particularly in his regimentals. He appears exactly as an officer ought to. Don't you think?" Fortunately, she continued without expecting an answer. "And he's so noble. He could be bitter and angry, but he's all amiability despite the horrible way he's been treated by—"

Darcy twisted his head around to glare at Kitty, whose mind finally caught up with her tongue.

"—by other people," she finished lamely.

Darcy immediately dismissed any consideration of telling Kitty the truth; her opinion was of no matter. But how could Elizabeth—? He had given her the letter. She knew the truth of Wickham's nature. Darcy had even revealed the truth about Georgiana. Elizabeth could not possibly trust the man.

But what if she had not read the letter?

Panic blazed through him like a lightning bolt. Writing a letter to an unmarried woman was highly improper, but Elizabeth had never seemed overly concerned about propriety. Had he shown a casual disregard for her reputation? Had he further provoked her rage? Perhaps she had never opened the letter. Perhaps she had thrown it into the fire.

He bit his tongue to stifle a cry of dismay.

I should not have quitted Kent without ensuring she would read the letter. His account of Georgiana's experience would have armed Elizabeth against Wickham, but why should she deign to read a letter from a man who had so thoroughly insulted her and her family? In all probability she had assumed the letter contained self-justifications or pleas for her to reconsider his proposal—and it had immediately been consigned to the fire.

Now she was in Brighton, believing that Wickham was a trustworthy man who had been wronged by Darcy.

Darcy rested his hand on the trunk of a nearby tree to keep his balance. "What have I done?" he whispered to himself.

"Mr. Darcy?" Kitty Bennet's face was screwed up with anxiety. "Are you about to be ill? You look so strange."

Good Lord, he had entirely forgotten her presence. "I believe something I ate may not have agreed with me." He touched his stomach briefly.

She backed away, saying in alarm, "My slippers are new."

"Perhaps we should return to the house," he said.

She nodded in fervent agreement. Darcy straightened his jacket and turned toward Longbourn. He needed to get to Brighton.

***

"Darcy, sit down. Simply watching you makes me restless!" Bingley complained as Darcy made his seventh or eighth lap across the drawing room floor, seemingly attempting to wear a path in Netherfield's carpet.

Darcy threw himself into a chair. "I should have departed tonight. Waiting was a mistake."

Bingley rolled his eyes. "Once again I remind you: the journey to Brighton is long—and dangerous on a moonless night."

"Imagine if Jane were in Brighton with that blackguard!" Darcy growled.

Bingley pressed his lips together until they turned white.

"He could compromise her—make her marry him. Or force himself upon her!" Unable to contain his energy, Darcy launched himself from the chair and resumed pacing.

"She is with Colonel Forster and his wife," Bingley pointed out for at least the third time. "They will protect her."

"Have you met the colonel's wife?" Darcy asked. "She may be all of eighteen years, and a strong wind would carry her away. She could not be trusted to protect Elizabeth from a sparrow."

"Well, the colonel is a level-headed man," Bingley said.

"He has other duties; he cannot watch her all the time." Darcy's hands clenched into fists as if preparing to fight.

Bingley shifted on the settee. "Have you considered your actions upon arriving in Brighton? You must have a plan. You did not part on the best of terms with Miss Elizabeth."

Darcy ran both hands through his hair. He had done nothing but think on that question in the past few hours but had discovered no satisfactory answer. "I will reason with her."

Bingley's brow furrowed. "She may not be disposed to heed your reasoning. If she refused to read your letter, she may refuse to listen to your words."

Darcy ground his teeth. Naturally this had occurred to him. "I will make her listen!" He could hear the desperation in his own voice. "She will not be able to ignore me."

"An auspicious beginning to a courtship," Bingley remarked dryly.

"Knowing the truth about George Wickham is more important," Darcy bit out. "More important than her feelings for me. Her safety is paramount."

"But surely you will agree it would be best if she were not further disaffected from you."

Darcy sighed. *What a muddle!* "Yes, of course."

"Have you considered that she might be in love with Wickham?" Bingley spoke slowly and carefully. "People in love can be blind."

Darcy had exerted tremendous effort to banish such thoughts. "She cannot be in love with Wickham!" he said savagely. Bingley said nothing, waiting for his friend to grow calmer. "But I can woo her away from Wickham."

Bingley raised an eyebrow. "Have you ever courted a woman before?"

"Of course."

"Ladies have pursued you. It is not precisely the same," his friend said with a grin.

"It cannot be that difficult," Darcy grumbled irritably.

"It would not be difficult if you were not the last man on earth she would ever consider marrying." Bingley shrugged.

Of course, Bingley was right. Who was Darcy fooling? He and Elizabeth had parted on the least amicable terms imaginable, following the world's most disastrous offer of marriage. Sinking back into his chair, Darcy closed his eyes and dropped his head. "I would welcome any advice you might have on the matter." He had no pride remaining when it came to Elizabeth Bennet.

After a moment Bingley shook his head. "I have none to offer, my friend. I have properly bungled my courtship with Jane."

"She appears to have forgiven you."

"Yes, as long as I make no more blunders."

Darcy would give anything to be in his friend's place.

"Are you certain you do not wish me to accompany you to Brighton?" Bingley asked.

The offer was tempting, but Darcy shook his head. "You must remain here and woo your lady. I will either stand or fall on my own merits." He fervently hoped she would listen to reason—that her future happiness did not rely on Darcy's paltry courtship skills.

"I have all the confidence in the world," Bingley said with a hearty smile. "Just be yourself."

Darcy snorted. "That is what created this mess."

Chapter Three

Three days was a long time to be constantly in Mr. Wickham's presence. Elizabeth had gained his trust, and he willingly passed time in her company; however, she had gained no useful information about his associates or the possible location of a hideout. Colonel Forster had cautioned her that gathering intelligence could be a tedious process requiring patience, but Elizabeth had still hoped for a quick conclusion to the proceedings. The sooner she learned Mr. Wickham's secrets, the sooner she could return home.

Brighton itself was pleasant enough. Elizabeth adored the beach, which she had visited only a handful of times. The town of Brighton offered a wide variety of diversions; indeed, the men of the regiment enjoyed so many balls, dinners, and card parties that she wondered when they could spare time to train.

However, other aspects of the visit were less pleasant. The discovery of Mr. Wickham's treachery made her more eager than ever to quit his company—at the precise moment when she could not do so. Elizabeth also wanted to remove Lydia from the influence of Mr. Wickham in particular, and militia officers in general. Absent even her parents' meager supervision, Lydia became even more flirtatious and outrageous. Elizabeth warned her youngest sister about the repercussions of unchecked behavior, but Lydia paid her scant attention, complaining that her older sister was "dull."

Today, as the men of the militia were to have rifle practice, Mrs. Forster had invited Elizabeth to accompany her and Lydia to the ladies' beach. Having no more useful occupation, Elizabeth accepted, reflecting that at least her sister could cause limited embarrassment at a beach that admitted no men.

Mrs. Forster was pretty, fashionable, and gracious in society, but she was…young. Elizabeth would guess her to be no older than eighteen, and she might very well be younger. For a married woman, her behavior was often just as silly as Lydia's. Elizabeth could not imagine what had possessed the steady and sober colonel to marry such a young and flighty woman, but she knew nothing of their situation. Perhaps the marriage had been arranged by their families. Or perhaps Colonel Forster simply admired a pretty face.

Although the colonel treated his wife affectionately, they spent little time in each other's company. Mrs. Forster was usually accompanied by a coterie of female friends and a not insignificant number of male admirers—primarily soldiers—with whom she flirted extravagantly. Elizabeth had previously observed such behavior in young married women. Since they were now attached, they believed themselves safe to inflict their most flirtatious impulses upon every unsuspecting man in the vicinity.

Elizabeth had been surprised at the invitation; she was hardly a favorite of Mrs. Forster's, and there were many flighty officers' wives in the town who could have accompanied the two women. However, as they walked down to the beach, she recalled that many of those women had expressed a great fear of the sea—particularly the prospect of being bitten by fish.

As they neared the beach, it became clear that the invitation had been at Lydia's instigation. She was excited to have a chance to try real sea bathing but also demonstrated substantial anxiety about the endeavor. Elizabeth had been to Ramsgate with her aunt and uncle Gardiner, so she was familiar with visits to the sea. But it was all new to Lydia, who slipped many glances at her older sister as if seeking reassurance. Elizabeth was secretly touched that her sister found her presence comforting.

Elizabeth had been silent during the walk as Lydia and Mrs. Forster dominated the conversation. First, the colonel's wife complained about the dreariness running a household on a militia salary—although she appeared to have a copious supply of jewels and gowns in the latest fashion. Then the conversation turned to who was in Brighton that week. Lydia was excited that the prince regent was in residence at the Marine Pavilion, but Mrs. Forster dashed the girl's hopes for encountering royalty. "The prince rarely leaves the Pavilion when he visits the town," she said with great authority. Lydia pouted, but Elizabeth thought it was just as well given what she knew of the prince.

As they drew closer to the beach, Lydia grew more visibly anxious, twisting her hands in the hem of her skirt. Finally, a question burst from her: "What if the fish nibble on my toes?"

Elizabeth laughed. "Ladies' toes are not in any fish's diet."

"But they might mistake my toes for a worm! Do fish have good eyesight?"

"I have been sea bathing many times," Mrs. Forster assured her. "And the fish have never paid me any heed."

Lydia considered this for a moment. "What about whales?"

"Whales?" Elizabeth asked.

"What if a whale swims up to the shore and swallows me whole? Like Jonah!"

"Then we shall add a new book to the Bible called the Book of Lydia," Elizabeth teased.

Lydia rolled her eyes. "Lizzy, I am in earnest! I shan't go in the water if there is any danger of whales."

Mrs. Forster gasped. "Oh dear, I never had the least thought about whales!"

Elizabeth took a deep breath for patience. "Whales cannot swim so close to land."

"Are you certain?" Lydia's fingers worried a bow on her dress.

"Quite certain. Whales are like big ships that sail across the ocean. If they come too close to land they will run aground."

Mrs. Forster tossed her head. She was very aware of Elizabeth's greater age and eagerly sought to assert her superiority as a married woman. "You must come sea bathing, Lydia! It is most healthful," she said with an air of great knowledge. "In *The Use of Seawater in the Diseases of the Glands*, Dr. Russell recommends regular sea bathing to treat many conditions."

Elizabeth had heard of the book, which had helped to prompt the popularity of sea bathing in England, but she was dubious about many of its claims. "Do you have diseased glands?" she asked.

Mrs. Forster raised her chin. "Regular sea bathing will keep them healthy."

"Quite a wise precaution," Elizabeth agreed.

Upon their arrival at the ladies' beach, Elizabeth repaired to a small hut to exchange her dress for a bathing costume: a simple long cotton shift. It would not conceal anything once it was wet; the fabric would cling to her limbs and grow transparent. Thank goodness men were not allowed at this beach!

Elizabeth emerged, enjoying the sensation of being unencumbered by skirts and petticoats but wishing she could swim unclothed as she did in the pond at Longbourn. Of course, the pond was very isolated, and she did not fear someone glimpsing her in her state of undress. The bathing costume was the best option for the beach, but Elizabeth still sighed regretfully at her long shift.

Their mother had not approved of swimming, so the younger girls had never accompanied Elizabeth and Jane to the pond. Her mother's disapproval had not deterred Elizabeth, and she had gone frequently enough to learn to swim.

When Elizabeth emerged from the hut, Lydia and Mrs. Forster were waiting for her; neither had changed their clothes. "Are you not bathing after all?" she asked them.

Mrs. Forster appeared confused. "Lydia and I will change in the bathing machine."

"Bathing machine?"

The other woman gestured toward the crowded beach. Several carriage-like contraptions stood in the shallow water. The door to one opened and a fully dressed but damp woman emerged and descended a few steps to the beach. Other bathing machines had rolled into the deeper water; bathers emerged through a door at the far end before being submerged in the sea.

"Oh!" Elizabeth had heard about bathing machines that allowed women to be "dipped" in the sea with the help of an attendant who ensured they did not drown. "I simply planned to swim."

Mrs. Forster gaped at her. "You know how to swim?" Elizabeth might as well have confessed to witchcraft.

"Yes."

The woman eyed the placid waves suspiciously. "Risk it if you wish! But Lydia and I shall use the bathing machine. I have secured the services of Martha Gunn herself!" She paused as though Elizabeth should be impressed.

"Very well," Elizabeth replied, neither knowing nor caring who Martha Gunn was.

"She is the most famous dipper in Brighton!" Lydia exclaimed, proud to know something her sister did not.

"What an odd profession," Elizabeth said to herself. But she mustered a smile for the other women. "How exciting! Please enjoy your sea bathing."

Elizabeth hurried toward the water while the other women approached one of the machines perched precariously on the beach. Mrs. Forster stopped to speak with great animation to a sturdy, florid-faced woman who stood beside the door. Mrs. Gunn presumably.

Most of the women on the beach wore casual morning clothes and sat on blankets, chatting and laughing. Some held parasols to shield their complexions from the sun while others walked about the beach collecting shells. Numerous women with damp and disordered hair attested to the popularity of the bathing machines.

Elizabeth made her way through the crowds to the edge of the water. The sand and smooth stones under her bare feet were warm, but not too hot. The cool water lapped around her feet as she waded deeper and deeper, up to her knees. Shielding her eyes from the bright sunlight, she gazed out to the horizon, enjoying the view of endless ocean.

There were only a few women, perhaps a dozen in all, who dared to experience the sea without the assistance of a bathing machine—and five were merely wading. However, a few women swam in earnest, including two who appeared to be naked.

Elizabeth waded deeper, gradually acclimating herself to the cooler temperature. It was most refreshing. When the water was deep enough, Elizabeth completely submerged herself, gasping slightly at the cold. The waves were mild; perfect conditions for swimming. Elizabeth swam back and forth, parallel to the shore, with strong, swift strokes. *How refreshing! I have passed far too much of my time recently in drawing rooms.* Already she was wondering when she would be able to return to the beach for a swim. How could such an outing be arranged?

Ultimately her muscles tired of the unaccustomed exercise, and Elizabeth returned to the shallower water. She stood in water to her waist as she caught her breath.

She had kept an eye on the bathing machine containing Lydia and Mrs. Forster. Now she noticed as it was pulled into deeper water by a weary horse.

Once the machine's back ramp was level with the water, one of the attendants freed the horse from its harness, walked it to the machine's other end, and attached it there. Clever. Such a system allowed them to return to shore without needing to turn the vehicle in a circle.

Mrs. Forster, dressed in her shift, emerged from the small door at the machine's end and sat on the protruding ramp, dangling her feet in the water. Without ceremony, Mrs. Gunn reached over and plucked the woman from the ramp. Goodness, she was strong! The dipper waded a little distance into deeper water and then dunked Mrs. Forster—one, two, three times—all the way into the water, carefully ensuring that even the top of her head and her feet were thoroughly soaked.

I suppose only a complete dunking will benefit the glands, Elizabeth thought.

Mrs. Forster emerged spluttering after each dunking, appearing quite bedraggled and miserable by the time Mrs. Gunn set her back on the machine's platform. *I wonder how much the colonel's wife paid for the privilege of being treated like a biscuit in a cup of tea?* Elizabeth found herself hoping that dipping did indeed have medicinal properties because the activity itself appeared to provide no obvious pleasure.

When it was Lydia's turn, Elizabeth's sister twitched and jerked. She searched the area as if seeking an escape, but there was nowhere to go. Noticing Lydia's disposition, Mrs. Gunn enlisted the help of the other attendant so that they formed a kind of chair with their arms to carry Lydia. But the youngest Miss Bennet screeched as though they were about to feed her to a wild animal. Completely ignoring Lydia's antics, the two women hastily dunked the squirming girl three times before depositing her again on the ramp.

As the machine rolled back to the beach, both women retreated into the interior where they would change their clothes.

After a few more minutes of swimming, Elizabeth emerged from the water. Lydia and Mrs. Forster had arrayed themselves on a blanket near the back of the beach—quite safe from hungry fish or whales. Although her hair was in disarray, Mrs. Forster was rosy-cheeked and animated. Perhaps her glands *had* improved.

However, Lydia was pale and unusually still. Elizabeth seated herself beside her sister. "Are you quite all right?"

Lydia made a disgusted face. "I swallowed some sea water. It tastes vile, but Mrs. Forster assures me it is quite healthful."

"Drinking sea water is healthful?" Elizabeth exclaimed. "I had not heard that. I do not like the taste either, and I give you permission not to consume it if you dislike it." Lydia's shoulders slumped in relief.

Several minutes passed while the ladies lounged on the blanket, enjoying the sunshine while Lydia recovered from her "ordeal." But soon Mrs. Forster jumped up to greet a passing friend. Quickly she was chatting with a constant stream of visitors—mostly wives of militia officers—who were walking along the beach or recuperating from their own sea bathing experiences. Lydia must have swallowed a great deal of sea water, for she made no effort to join the gossipers despite casting them some longing glances.

Lydia grimaced when one woman spoke particularly loudly; Elizabeth frowned at her quizzically. "I don't like that Mrs. Morton," Lydia said in a low voice. "She is always flirting with Wicky."

"Wicky?" Elizabeth repeated blankly.

Lydia rolled her eyes. "Wickham. She flirts shamelessly, but anyone can see he doesn't care for her at all."

Elizabeth had been awaiting an opportunity to discuss Mr. Wickham with her sister. "Lydia, I do not believe Mr. Wickham is an entirely respectable companion for a girl of your age. You should exercise caution in his presence."

Lydia lifted her chin. "That would suit you, wouldn't it? When you are trying to steal him away from me."

Elizabeth gaped. "Steal him away? He has never demonstrated any partiality for you."

Lydia made an undignified squawk. "He danced two dances with me at the last ball, and the other day he said my bonnet was quite becoming!"

Good grief! Mr. Wickham would flirt with a dog—at least a female dog. "Mr. Denny danced two dances with you as well, and he was very complimentary about your gown." Perhaps Elizabeth could direct Lydia's attention in a safer direction; Wickham's friend at least was not a traitor to the crown—as far as Elizabeth knew.

Lydia made a little moue of disgust. "Denny is nice enough, I suppose. But he isn't a gentleman. Not like Wickham."

I must be more direct. "Mr. Wickham is not a gentleman either. He has gambling debts—serious debts. He told us many untruths about his relationship with Mr. Darcy, who never treated him unfairly at all. Quite the contrary."

"Lizzy!" Lydia squeaked. "I thought you liked Wicky! I cannot believe you would devise such falsehoods about him."

"I am telling you the truth." Elizabeth spoke through gritted teeth.

Lydia put her hands on her hips. "Then why do you flirt with him?"

Elizabeth would not have described her actions as flirting, but it was unsurprising Lydia viewed them in that light. "I am not flirting; I am simply being friendly."

"I have never seen you be so 'friendly' with any man!" Lydia exclaimed.

Elizabeth let out an exasperated sigh. If only she could explain the truth! But Lydia could not be trusted to keep such a secret. "Believe me, Lydia, I have no aspirations to make Mr. Wickham my beau. He is far too—" She just barely prevented herself from uttering the word "dangerous." "—too unstable. You should not get close to him."

Lydia tossed her head. "You are not Papa. You cannot tell me what to do. Wicky likes me better than you anyway. And I shall prove it!"

With that declaration, Lydia climbed to her feet and hurried to join the cluster of people conversing with Mrs. Forster. Elizabeth did not follow; they could not continue such a conversation in front of others.

She was unsurprised that Lydia had not heeded her warning, but she had hoped to at least give her sister cause for reflection where the man was concerned. Elizabeth sighed; she would simply have to watch her sister carefully around the militia officer.

At the moment there was nothing to do but savor the sights and smells of the seaside. Waves rolling onto the beach created a hypnotic rhythm. The sun was bright, but a brisk breeze kept it from being too warm. Growing drowsy, Elizabeth slid down on the blanket until her head was pillowed on her arms, and she fell asleep.

The sun was past its zenith when she awoke; Elizabeth judged it to be early afternoon. Her stomach reminded her forcefully that she had not enjoyed any luncheon. Perhaps she could persuade the other women to return to the house for some refreshments.

Sitting up, she shaded her eyes to scan the beach, which had fewer inhabitants than earlier. Lydia was fast asleep on the blanket beside Elizabeth, snoring lightly. But Mrs. Forster was nowhere visible. She was not walking on the beach or talking with any of the women Elizabeth could see. It was possible she was in one of the bathing machines trundling deeper into the water, but would the colonel's wife subject herself to such treatment twice in one day?

Elizabeth stood, shaking sand from her shift, and surveyed the beach more fully. There still was no sign of Mrs. Forster. Would the woman have returned home and left them sleeping on the beach?

She climbed up a slight incline of piled sand, heading toward the grassy area near the road. Perhaps Mrs. Forster had taken a stroll along the street in search of refreshment. Rounding the corner behind a cluster of small huts, Elizabeth located her quarry. Several yards away, Mrs. Forster was in urgent conversation with Mr. Wickham.

Elizabeth quickly hid behind the huts. Mrs. Forster might be sufficiently clad, but Elizabeth wore only a shift, and Mr. Wickham was the last man she wished to see her so attired. *Why is he so close to the ladies' beach? Is he hoping to catch a glimpse of partially clad bathing beauties? If he is only indulging his prurient curiosity, why is Mrs. Forster allowing it?*

The two conversed quietly, their heads together and Mr. Wickham's hand on Mrs. Forster's arm in a rather familiar way. With all his attention on the woman beside him, he made no effort to spy on the ladies' beach. A row of trees would conceal them from the sight of nearly everyone on the beach or street. Unfortunately, Elizabeth could not approach the couple and listen to their conversation without being observed.

Before they could notice her, Elizabeth hurried back to the blanket, considering the import of what she had seen. Mrs. Forster flirted with every man in the regiment. It flustered some officers, and many ignored it, but Mr. Wickham seemed to enjoy the attention and returned her flirtatious banter. Such was the nature of their characters that Elizabeth had thought little of it. Today, however, they had conversed intimately in a location that would conceal them from sight. Were they conducting an affair?

Elizabeth gasped at the thought. Mr. Wickham was younger and far more handsome than Colonel Forster; she would not be the first wife to stray from an older husband. But Mrs. Forster would take a terrible risk by forming an intimate relationship with another officer. If the colonel discovered them, Mr. Wickham would lose his position and could be brought up on charges. Dallying with other officers' wives was strictly forbidden. The colonel could sue his wife for divorce if she had been unfaithful. Quite a scandal would ensue.

Taking her place on the blanket beside the still-slumbering Lydia, Elizabeth wondered if she should mention her suspicion to the colonel. But what could she say? That Mr. Wickham was at the ladies' beach? That might earn him a mild reprimand. Without seeing how intimately the two had stood, the colonel might not understand her concern. Their conversation was probably completely innocent but conducted in a flirtatious manner. Most likely any report would only cause the colonel heartache, sowing doubt without providing any certainty.

Elizabeth's mission was to observe Mr. Wickham for *treasonous* activities; she had not been asked to concern herself with the state of the colonel's marriage. He might not thank her for any interference. Yes, it would be best not to say anything.

Chapter Four

Darcy thought he might be ill.

Upon arriving in Brighton, he had secured lodgings at the Crescent, one of the more elegant buildings in town. His next task had been to call upon Colonel Forster and hopefully Elizabeth. The hour was rather late in the afternoon for a call, but he could not bring himself to wait until the morrow. Elizabeth and Wickham had already been in Brighton for four days without his supervision.

The colonel's lodgings were on the corner of two streets not far from the beach. It was not the most fashionable neighborhood but eminently suitable for a militia officer. As Darcy strode up a side street toward the front entrance, he happened to get a glimpse into the garden, where someone had carelessly left the rear gate open. This provided Darcy with an unobstructed view of…Elizabeth sitting with Wickham on a garden bench.

The sight had struck fear in Darcy's heart, and he had stifled an impulse to remove Wickham bodily from Elizabeth's vicinity. Instead, he reminded himself it was an opportunity to gather more information about Wickham's intentions. Even while berating himself that such devious activities were beneath him, Darcy had stolen closer, peering through a hole in the fence.

What he saw nearly made him toss up his accounts on the dirt of the back alley. Elizabeth and Wickham sat side by side on a wrought iron bench before a low rose bush, facing a weeping willow tree. However, neither appeared to be appreciating the garden's beauty. Wickham spoke with great animation, although Darcy could not discern the words. Elizabeth regarded him with rapt attention, a soft smile on her lips. Worse, she clung to one of Wickham's hands with both of hers while he gesticulated vigorously with the other.

The sight sickened Darcy, and yet he could not tear his eyes away. In the weeks since he had seen Elizabeth, he had done his best to convince himself that his memories exaggerated her beauty. But in truth, memory had not done Elizabeth justice. Soft, dark curls fell around her face, and the faintest tinge of pink colored her cheeks. Her deep emerald gown echoed the sea green color in her eyes. Darcy would gladly have admired her all day.

However, he did not like the besotted expression on her face. Darcy would have given his entire fortune if she would direct such an expression of adoration at him. Seeing it bestowed upon such an unworthy recipient was…provoking another bout of nausea.

The low murmur of feminine voices alleviated Darcy's anxiety that the pair was alone. Solitude would give opportunities for many kinds of mischief, but the colonel's wife and a few women were nearby. However, Wickham behaved as if they were unchaperoned, taking Elizabeth's hand and brushing it with his lips.

Pressing his eye to the hole in the fence, Darcy clenched his fists until his knuckles turned white. More than anything he wanted to race into the garden and wipe Wickham's cocky smile from his face with a well-placed right hook. But a violent reaction would only provoke sympathy for Wickham and confirm Elizabeth's worst opinion about Darcy.

Even as Darcy observed, Elizabeth laughed—a high shrill sound he had never heard her make. Nor had he ever glimpsed such adoration on her face. She always spoke to Darcy with an arch and teasing manner, with glances full of cleverness and understanding.

Why was her manner so different with Wickham? How was it possible? Was Wickham the one she wanted? Had she rejected Darcy because of her infatuation with the militia officer? Perhaps she was so besotted with the man that she simply had not believed a word of Darcy's letter.

Darcy's stomach threatened rebellion once more, and he focused his thoughts on not disgracing himself—the better to avoid a sense of grief that threatened to engulf him and drag him to the bottom of the ocean. If Wickham were the one she wanted, if she were infatuated with the man, then it was possible she was not the person Darcy believed her to be. His heart contracted painfully. He had not thought it possible to feel worse after her rejection in Hunsford, but this sight was proving him wrong.

Additional activity in the garden drew Darcy from his musings. Wickham whispered in Elizabeth's ear while she simpered and edged closer to him on the bench. His smile held a hint of a smirk. She was completely fooled, and he knew it; he was enjoying the charade.

I have been a fool. Well, that was not news—not since Hunsford. But now he was recognizing new depths to his foolishness. Not only had Darcy deceived himself about Elizabeth's feelings, but he had also mistaken her character—and even her judgment.

Why was she so blind to Wickham's lies? Surely she had burned Darcy's letter. Damnation!

Darcy turned away from the sickening sight in the garden to stare at the cobblestones of Church Street. He would retreat to his lodgings, pack his belongings, and return to London. No one would ever know he had been to Brighton—after he swore Bingley to secrecy. He would leave Elizabeth to the consequences of her own folly. She was not the woman he had believed her to be, and thus she was not the right woman for him.

Perhaps she was not capable of loving Darcy. If she preferred a man like Wickham—handsome, smooth, and easy of manner—someone like Darcy would never satisfy her. Darcy's hand shook violently where it grasped the edge of the fence, and his eyes burned. *I must escape now*, he warned himself, *before someone notices me, and I disgrace myself further*.

The street beckoned, offering a quick escape. He could leave Brighton today and find some coaching inn on the road where he could get utterly foxed. Forget about Elizabeth…for a time.

Yet he could not bring his fingers to release the wood of the fence—nor compel his feet to walk toward the street. He could not abandon Elizabeth to her fate. *I am pathetic. She has rejected me. She is not the woman I thought her to be. And yet I cannot let her go.*

Oh, he could tell himself that he was being chivalrous or that he felt responsible for not warning her family about Wickham—both of those things were true. But the real truth was that—despite evidence of her lack of discernment and her infatuation with another man—Darcy was still desperately in love with Elizabeth. Perhaps the sight in the garden should have altered his sentiments, but it had not. Not one whit.

His only solace was that nobody knew the depths of his shame. He must take care to keep it that way.

He wheeled around, again peering through the hole in the fence to torture himself with the sight of Wickham whispering into Elizabeth's ear while she giggled. Giggled! Had Darcy ever provoked a giggle from Elizabeth? He was quite sure he would never touch food again.

But he could not abandon her to Wickham's clutches. She might not be his, but he still must save her from Wickham. Even if he could not win her love, he could thwart Wickham's plans and keep Elizabeth safe. That must be enough.

But how could he rescue her from the blackguard?

Paralyzed without an answer to this question, Darcy was a horrified witness as Wickham kissed his way up Elizabeth's bare arm while she giggled and blushed with pleasure. The officer skimmed over the puffed muslin sleeve of her dress and stole a few kisses along her collarbone and the long pale column of her neck.

Then his lips brushed hers. Once. Twice.

Darcy slapped his hand over his mouth against the impulse to roar his outrage. He wanted to race into the garden and tear Wickham bodily from the woman he loved. *Those should be my hands on her skin! My lips brushing hers!* Darcy wanted to punch Wickham, but he equally wanted to punish himself. *Why could I not make her giggle and blush in such a way?*

Fortunately for the state of Darcy's nerves, Elizabeth demurred, turning her head away from Wickham and murmuring something softly, her hand resting at her throat. Wickham nodded and pulled away. Her discomfort with such intimacy was a slight balm to Darcy's heart.

He watched the couple converse for a few more minutes, but then Elizabeth rose and called out to the other women in the garden. They answered, and soon—thankfully— Elizabeth and Wickham had disappeared into the house.

Darcy could not have borne another minute. *I am the last man in the world she would marry, and yet she allows this wastrel to kiss her!* Darcy's heart had been flayed with a whip.

He waited a moment for his jagged heartbeat to slow and for his hands to cease shaking. Then he silently picked his way through the refuse strewn about the alley and hurried back to his lodgings. He had plans to make.

***

Darcy spent the remainder of the afternoon pacing the floor of his elegant rooms in the Crescent. The carpet in both the bedroom and sitting room was quite lush—an exotic oriental pattern of some kind. After hours of perambulation, Darcy was intimately familiar with the pattern and not much closer to a plan for how he might rescue Elizabeth from Wickham.

At first he considered writing another letter about his dealings with Wickham but immediately discarded the idea. An unguarded moment to transfer such a missive was unlikely to occur, and he had no reason to believe she would read a second letter. No need to provide additional kindling for her fire.

He might also relate the story in person, but they would need a reasonable degree of privacy given the sensitive subject. Georgiana's reputation could not be jeopardized by sharing the tale before others. Obtaining any time alone with Elizabeth would not be a simple matter. He did not expect her to be pleased at his sudden appearance in Brighton, and she would not be inclined to grant him a solitary audience. He fully anticipated that even public attempts to speak with her would be…awkward.

And he had experienced enough awkward encounters with Elizabeth Bennet to last him a lifetime.

Darcy had considered and discarded many other schemes, including reporting Wickham's debts to his superior officer, arranging for Wickham to be posted elsewhere, or even—in desperation—challenging the man to a duel. But any of those actions were likely to provoke Elizabeth's sympathy for the blackguard and her antipathy toward Darcy.

Clenching his fist, Darcy thumped the wall. Damn Wickham for being so insufferably likeable! He charmed wherever he went, pleasing everyone with his manners and wit. In his younger days, Darcy had longed for one-quarter of Wickham's easy ways with people; now he had accepted that he would always be doomed to be awkward in company. At least his fortune compensated for his lack of ease—until he met the one woman who was indifferent to his fortune.

How could he convince her of Wickham's perfidy? If they were simply friends, he might find some way to convince her, but they were not even that.

I myself am the biggest obstacle. Elizabeth does not like me.

She considered him offensive, unmannerly, and—the deepest cut of all—ungentlemanlike.

Also, he was the last person in the world she would consider marrying. But at this point he would settle for having her ear.

How could he persuade her to listen to him when she disliked him so intensely? After his farce of a proposal, she would undoubtedly avoid his presence. He cringed recalling how he had insulted her family, condescended to find her attractive, and confessed he loved her against his will. He was fortunate indeed that she had not slapped his face.

Perhaps she would listen to the story about Wickham if someone else told it? Maybe Richard? No, his cousin was ten times more charming than Darcy himself, who hardly needed more competition for Elizabeth's attention. Furthermore, Richard could not be in Brighton for days.

Darcy slumped in a chair. *I must find a way to warn her about Wickham. But how will I speak with her alone? And how do I ensure she will believe my story?*

Pushing himself from the chair, he resumed pacing—then stopped as a horrible thought struck him, paralyzing him in the middle of the room. *Wickham might make Elizabeth an offer of marriage. I can do nothing to prevent it.*

No, surely not. Elizabeth had no dowry to speak of, nothing to tempt Wickham. Unless the man was aware of Darcy's interest in her…and made her an offer just to spite his childhood rival. Darcy bit down on his knuckles to stifle a moan. How would he bear it?

But surely Wickham remained unaware of Darcy's interest. He had been discreet with his attentions to Elizabeth in Hertfordshire.

Was it possible Elizabeth might tell Wickham about the marriage proposal? Darcy's knees threatened to collapse, and he grabbed the back of a chair to prevent a fall. *Had they laughed together over tales of my inept proposal?* Darcy's stomach threatened rebellion again. *No, Elizabeth is an honorable woman; she would not betray my trust.*

Unless he had been completely deceived in her character. If that were the case, all of Darcy's efforts were for naught.

No, he would not venture down that road.

However, Wickham might have guessed Darcy's interest in Meryton, and Elizabeth might have dropped some inadvertent hints. It was possible that Wickham might make Elizabeth an offer purely to thwart Darcy. Despite the warmth in the room, Darcy shivered as he realized he had a bigger dilemma than he had initially thought.

How could he prevent it?

Darcy emitted a mirthless chuckle. At Rosings, he would have assumed that the obvious solution was to propose himself since he was presumably a more palatable alternative than Wickham. In the days since the Hunsford disaster, Darcy had gradually realized how little he had considered or attempted to understand Elizabeth's feelings. Assuming she was in love with him, Darcy had believed his fortune would overcome whatever reservations she might experience about the match.

The irony did not escape him. For years he had fled fortune hunters, and yet he had expected his fortune to be the primary enticement for matrimony.

Still, there was only one way to prevent her from marrying Wickham: marry her himself.

He could not help picturing the Netherfield drawing room and hearing Bingley's voice asking if Darcy had ever wooed a lady. He had never considered it to be an ability he should develop, but suddenly Elizabeth's future happiness depended upon it.

Perhaps he could begin their renewed acquaintance with an apology. Yes, here was a sound strategy. If she believed in his contrition, she might grant Darcy an opportunity to court her. Given the chance, he might convince her how deeply he cared about her.

But how? She did not even like him.

Blast and damnation! This love business was so much more complicated than he had anticipated. How did other men go about winning wives?

They wooed them. They courted them. They gave them flowers and flirted and paid compliments about their hair and gowns. Darcy had believed he was above such foolishness, but Elizabeth had shown him that his sense of superiority was precisely the problem.

Darcy stopped pacing, staring at the egregious still life on the far wall. *What would happen if I did court Elizabeth? I could flirt, dance with her, bring her flowers, and offer compliments. I could woo her away from Wickham.*

But what did he know about courting a woman? His one attempt had ended with the woman declaring he was the last man she would ever marry. His courtship efforts could only be counted as an abject failure.

He had believed she was flirting with him when, in fact, she had hated him. If her future happiness depended on Darcy's ability to woo her effectively, she was surely doomed.

It seemed such a hopeless case that he might as well give up now, but his stomach knotted with tension at that thought. There was no alternative; he *must* draw her away from Wickham. If Darcy did not court Elizabeth, she might be shackled to a worthless blackguard for the rest of her life. He could not allow that to happen.

Perhaps I am inept at courtship, but surely I may learn. I am clever; I may show her I have attended to her reproaches and corrected my behavior. My understanding of Elizabeth has improved as well. He could woo her more effectively now—could he not?

He also possessed one great advantage over Wickham: he actually loved Elizabeth. When she compared the two men, hopefully she would perceive the sincerity of Darcy's sentiments.

Further, wealth was an advantage in courtship. He could give her gifts, take her for carriage rides, show her sights—woo her in ways Wickham could not manage. It would scarcely be a hardship to spend more time with her. Perhaps he could manage to improve her opinion of him. Maybe even make her fall in love with him…

No, that was too much to hope.

Still, some of her dislike was based on misapprehension and mistake. He could demonstrate that he was not always proud and difficult. He could exert himself to be charming and have pleasing manners. Even if he could not win her hand, he would be in a better position to thwart Wickham's influence and prevent—God forbid—an elopement.

Of course, if he failed, he might drive her straight into Wickham's arms. Best not to think about that.

Chapter Five

Perhaps I should consider a career on the stage once my life as a spy comes to an end, Elizabeth thought. Apparently, Mr. Wickham was wholly convinced of her infatuation with him even though every flicker of his smile caused her stomach to clench with dread.

How did I ever find his manners pleasing? Why did I believe him to be amiable and honorable?

She was ashamed at her own lack of perspicacity. Now armed with superior knowledge of the man, she scrutinized his every gesture and statement. His air of casual charm was the result of elaborate effort, and he probably uttered fewer than ten sincere words in a day.

Knowing he had no honor, Elizabeth found it almost painful to watch him ingratiate himself—and to witness others respond in good faith. A thousand small clues now became apparent. He acted self-effacing yet somehow always managed to get his own way. He claimed not to wish to speak ill of anyone yet was one of the most vicious gossipmongers she had ever met.

It shook her to think how readily she had been deceived, recalling how she had taken Mr. Wickham's part with Mr. Darcy. After he had declared his love, she had vilified the man's character based on lies this scoundrel had told her. How she had wronged him! He was indeed proud and difficult but had always behaved honorably.

With these thoughts swirling through her head, Elizabeth found it difficult to even manage a smile for Mr. Wickham as he oozed his way through the crush of people at Lord and Lady Cavendish's ball. Everyone succumbed to the Wickham mystique. They smiled as he passed and readily gave way. The men grasped him by the arm to speak with him while women—even those who were married—simpered and fluttered their lashes. Indeed, he was handsome, but could nobody guess what a rogue he was? Enjoying the attention, Mr. Wickham smiled and laughed freely. Why would he not? Everyone in Brighton loved him.

In Elizabeth's mind, the necessity of behaving as one of his admirers compounded the evil of his deception. As she laughed at his jokes and fluttered her eyelashes at him, she felt complicit with his deceit.

Despite Elizabeth's admonishments, Lydia was firmly among Mr. Wickham's many admirers. When the gentleman showed a marked preference for Elizabeth's company, Lydia complained, pouted, or flirted more outrageously. In company, she passed nearly as much time glaring at Elizabeth as she did admiring the officer. If only she knew how little Elizabeth enjoyed his attentions!

At least if he focuses his attentions on me, he pays less heed to Lydia and decreases the risk he might damage her reputation. The possible damage to Elizabeth's reputation, however, was best not dwelt upon.

Her smile was firmly in place by the time Mr. Wickham reached her side. They had already danced one set, and she gritted her teeth knowing she must acquiesce to a second. He executed a small bow. "Miss Elizabeth, would you do me the honor of another—?"

"There you are, Lizzy!" Lydia, boisterous and possibly foxed, burst upon them and grabbed Elizabeth's arm as though they had not seen one another for a fortnight. Then she affected to notice the officer. "Here you are, Wicky! I believe you promised me a dance!"

Elizabeth turned a laugh into a cough; a blind man would have noticed the transparency of her sister's maneuver.

"Did I?" Mr. Wickham smirked.

"Indeed, and it would be quite a scandal if you did not keep your word!" Lydia peeked coyly from under her lashes.

I hope nobody is observing this exchange. Lydia was too forward; a woman never asked a gentleman to dance, and such behavior would do her reputation no good. "Mr. Wickham requested the next set with me," Elizabeth informed Lydia. It was not quite true, but he certainly had been about to make the request.

Mr. Wickham did not dispute the assertion but held out his arm for her. Elizabeth managed not to shrink away in disgust as she took it.

Lydia pouted charmingly. "But Lizzy already danced with you." She turned a far less charming expression on her sister. "Let me have my turn." Lydia looped her arm through the man's other arm, taking possession of his left while Elizabeth had his right.

"Come, Wicky!" Lydia said brightly, tugging him toward the dance floor.

Loath to encourage such forwardness, Elizabeth ground her teeth and tugged him in the opposite direction. "You may dance with him later," she told Lydia.

Such feminine attention delighted Mr. Wickham. "Ladies, ladies, there is enough of me to share!" he declared as he scanned the room to see who noticed this evidence of his desirability.

"You had a turn with him!" Lydia declared to her sister, jerking the man toward her and causing his head to snap to one side.

The commotion was attracting attention, and Elizabeth was tempted to relinquish a prize she truly did not desire. But her charade necessitated that she maintain a pretense of infatuation with the officer. *The things I do for my country.*

Tugging on the gentleman's other arm, she murmured, "Lydia, you are making a spectacle!"

Lydia yanked in the opposite direction, causing the man's head to wobble back and forth like a doll's. Mr. Denny approached with a tentative expression on his face. A fellow officer and friend of Mr. Wickham's, Mr. Denny was young and eager to please.

"Might I be of service?" he asked with a shy smile. "Miss Lydia, I would be honored if you danced with me." But Lydia ignored him.

"Be reasonable," Elizabeth pleaded with her sister.

Lydia sneered. "Why must I always be the reasonable one? Perhaps you could be 'reasonable' for once!"

Apparently weary of the tug-of-Wickham, the officer finally pulled his arm from Lydia's grasp. "I am honored to have caught the eye of two such beautiful women," he said, preening, "but Miss Lydia, I have promised this set to your sister. I would be honored to dance the next set with you."

Lydia stamped her foot and scowled. "Very well! I am certain *Denny* will be happy to dance this set with me." Flouncing over to the other officer, she practically thrust her hand into his. More than a little besotted with Lydia, Denny beamed at her drunkenly until she sighed in exasperation and pulled him toward the dancers.

"I apologize for Lydia's inappropriate behavior," Elizabeth said to Mr. Wickham, not needing to feign her embarrassment.

The man straightened the cuff of his coat. "That is quite all right." He flashed her a grin full of white teeth. His obvious enjoyment of the spectacle made Elizabeth feel a little queasy. "Shall we join the set?"

As he led her to the dance floor, Elizabeth reflected that never before had she won a contest when she had so little desire for the prize.

***

An hour later, Elizabeth had finished the second of her two obligatory dance sets with Mr. Wickham—devoutly wishing she could also be relieved of the burden of pretending an interest in his company.

She had paced the edges of the ballroom while he danced with Lydia, unable to leave her sister unsupervised. When Elizabeth joined the pair immediately after the conclusion of the set, Lydia pouted. Elizabeth feared the onset of another tug-of-Wickham, but upon discovering a tear in one of her flounces, Lydia hastened to the ladies' retiring room.

Expressing an interest in lemonade won her a brief reprieve from Mr. Wickham's presence, but he reappeared all too soon, deftly juggling two full glasses. He handed one to her with a smile that was no doubt intended to be alluring. "Your wish is my command, my lady."

"You are all that is gracious," Elizabeth responded, avoiding any touch of his fingers as she took her glass.

His smile transformed into a smirk. "Would that I could have another dance with you."

She tried to appear coy. "That would occasion too much talk."

He took a step toward her, standing closer than was entirely appropriate. "Let them talk about us." His breath ghosted over her face, and she closed her eyes lest her disgust register on her countenance.

Remember your mission. If she was forced to spend time with the man, at least she could ensure that it was valuable. Casting a demure glance at the floor, Elizabeth stepped away from the officer. "I would prefer not to be the subject of gossip, but perhaps we might take a turn about the room?"

"Capital idea!" After transferring their lemonade glasses to a passing servant, Wickham offered his arm and led her on a stately stroll around the perimeter of the ballroom.

Elizabeth broke the silence first. "Do you have a wide acquaintance in Brighton, sir?"

Mr. Wickham flashed a smile. "Of course! I have friends wherever I go. There is my friend, Henry Knox, from my days at Cambridge. He's hereabouts somewhere." The officer made a vague gesture. "And Edward Plummer. I know him from Derbyshire. He and his wife were invited but could not attend." Elizabeth tried to memorize these names. "Lord Cavendish is a friend as well."

Elizabeth bounced on her toes. "If they are as pleasant as you, I would love to meet some of your friends!"

"No one is as pleasant as I am," Mr. Wickham said with a devilish grin.

"To be sure." Elizabeth laughed. "But you always discover the most amiable and amusing people wherever you are."

The officer puffed out his chest. "Have you been introduced to Lord Cavendish?"

"A real lord?" she echoed breathlessly. "No, but I would find it most agreeable."

Mr. Wickham's grin was as condescending as Elizabeth could expect. "We are quite well acquainted already, having met over several games of cards."

"I would be honored," she breathed. Abandoning the perimeter, Mr. Wickham led her across the ballroom to the entrance where Lord and Lady Cavendish greeted new arrivals. Their guests were a varied lot, including many men in red uniforms as well as members of the local gentry and prosperous merchants. Mr. Wickham wove them through the throng until they stood at Lord Cavendish's elbow.

"Lord Cavendish, may I present Miss Elizabeth Bennet?"

The lord eyed her like something he had found on the sole of his shoe. When his eyes drifted over Mr. Wickham, his face displayed only a vague recognition. Elizabeth hid a smirk.

"We met over cards two days ago," Mr. Wickham prompted.

"Ah, yes, Wyndham." Somehow the lord managed to speak while barely moving his lips, as if they were barely worth the effort of speech. Well, at least the lord was not one of Mr. Wickham's co-conspirators.

The officer maintained his amiable smile. "Wickham."

The lord nodded absently as his attention was drawn to the door. "If you will forgive me, I must greet my guests." He took a step forward, smiling at the man entering the room. "Darcy, I am so pleased you could come!"

Startled, Elizabeth and Mr. Wickham simultaneously turned toward Fitzwilliam Darcy as he strolled into the ballroom, effortlessly elegant in an impeccably tailored suit of blue and gold. While the master of Pemberley exchanged pleasantries with their host, his eyes ranged over Elizabeth and Mr. Wickham, narrowing slightly when he noticed their linked arms. But he betrayed no surprise. *Did he know I would be here with Mr. Wickham?*

It seemed unlikely. How could he? No, his presence must be a coincidence.

Mr. Darcy was the last person she would have expected to encounter in Brighton; she had fully expected never to see him again. Growing hot beneath his scrutiny, she fought the impulse to avert her eyes from the man. What must he think of her?

Baring his soul to her, Mr. Darcy had revealed Mr. Wickham's responsibility for his sister's near disgrace. Now he found her on that man's arm! He must think her the world's greatest simpleton—or a woman without any moral qualms whatsoever.

Mr. Darcy stared at her as if the rest of the room had ceased to exist; the intensity of his gaze could almost burn a hole in her skull. Noting the sudden unease in the air, Lord Cavendish stepped back and gestured to them awkwardly. "Allow me to introduce Mr. Wyndham and Miss—"

Mr. Darcy stepped forward and bowed. "Bennet," he finished. "A pleasure, as always." He did not smile, but his gaze would not leave her face. He had not even acknowledged Mr. Wickham.

"You are acquainted?" The lord seemed a bit surprised that Mr. Darcy would have such low connections.

"Indeed," Mr. Darcy said smoothly. "Miss Bennet and I encountered each other not long ago when I was visiting my aunt in Kent." Although he was responding to their host's question, his words were aimed at Mr. Wickham, who stiffened and frowned at this information.

As an awkward silence settled over the group, Elizabeth felt compelled to address Mr. Darcy. "I did not know you had plans to visit Brighton."

"I had no such plans in April, but recently I had a sudden urge to enjoy some sea bathing while the water is still warm."

"Of course." Elizabeth responded automatically, although she did not believe this explanation. Mr. Darcy was not the sort of man to indulge in any sea bathing, let alone to conceive a sudden desire for it.

Mr. Wickham bestowed on Mr. Darcy a smile that was little more than bared teeth. Lord Cavendish had been observing the trio in bemusement but was then summoned away by his wife. Barely acknowledging their host's departure, Mr. Darcy regarded Elizabeth steadily. "Miss Bennet, I have not had the pleasure of dancing with you since the Netherfield ball. I see a new set is forming. Would you do me the honor?"

"Uh…er…" How had the English language deserted her in her hour of need?

"See here now, Darcy!" Mr. Wickham exclaimed. "She is engaged to dance with me."

I am caught between two men who hate each other—and I wish to dance with neither. What a disaster. "We have already danced two sets,

Mr. Wickham," she reminded the officer, who glowered while Mr. Darcy raised a triumphant brow.

"Shall we?" Mr. Darcy gestured to the dance floor.

Elizabeth could think of no suitable reason to decline the offer. She could hardly claim an injured ankle now. "Yes, thank you."

With a rather grim smile, Mr. Darcy offered his arm, which she took reluctantly. Scowling, Mr. Wickham stalked toward the punch table where Mr. Denny spoke with a few other officers.

As Mr. Darcy drew her toward the dancers, she wondered at his behavior. She had believed she had driven him from her life at Hunsford. Yet here he was, treating her with great amiability. Was his friendliness a ruse so that later he might disparage her want of decorum? No, surely he would not be so petty.

His smile had dropped away, and he viewed her solemnly from under lowered brows. Was he angry at finding her on Mr. Wickham's arm? Foolish question. Of course, he was—angry and disappointed. Mr. Wickham had blackened Mr. Darcy's name and nearly ruined his sister.

How could she possible justify her friendliness toward the scoundrel now? He might think she had disregarded his letter—or disbelieved it. She hated that he might think the worst of her. How she longed to explain her behavior, but she had promised the colonel she would tell no one.

Her hands shook, and perspiration dripped down her neck; she could not meet his eyes. Of all the people in England, Mr. Darcy was the one who would least expect her to behave charitably toward Mr. Wickham. For some reason she could not fathom, she found that she did not desire his ill opinion.

The music commenced, but being at the end of the row, they awaited their turn to dance. The muscles in Mr. Darcy's jaw twitched, as if he wished to speak but feared saying the wrong words. "I was surprised to find you in Mr. Wickham's company," he said finally.

Elizabeth lifted her chin. *I am on the crown's business; I cannot allow anyone to intimidate me*, she reminded herself. There was no choice but to brazen it out, but the thought of Mr. Darcy's disappointment made her heartsick. "Oh?"

"Yes, I thought better of your discernment." The words were uttered without bitterness, yet they struck Elizabeth with the force of arrows shot from a bow.

Hopefully the mortification was not displayed on her face. Now she would be forced to defend the officer's character while secretly agreeing with Mr. Darcy's assessment of him. "Mr. Wickham is an amiable companion and an accomplished dancer."

No. I owe this man no explanations, she reminded herself. She *had* been deceived about Mr. Wickham's character, but Mr. Darcy had still been rude and unpleasant in making his offer of marriage. "I see no harm in dancing with him." She forced herself to raise her eyes and meet his.

Mr. Darcy's face was white, and he squeezed her hand so tightly it hurt. "He is a blackguard of the first order! He does not deserve your—!" He bit off the last word and turned his head, clearly in the grip of violent emotion.

Elizabeth needed to turn the conversation away from a subject where she was so vulnerable. "If we pass the set discussing Mr. Wickham's failings, it will be a solemn dance indeed," she said with a playful tone. "Was that your intention in asking me to dance?"

He blinked. "No, of course not."

In the next moment the dancing commenced, and they fell silent as they focused on the intricate movements of the piece. When they next came together, Mr. Darcy seemed to have mastered his agitation, regarding her with a more serene countenance. "Are you enjoying Brighton?"

"I like it very much. The seaside is quite beautiful."

"Have you been sea bathing?"

"Yes. I found it is quite different from swimming in a pond."

"You know how to swim?" His eyebrows rose.

"There is a small pond on our property where I have been swimming many times with my sister." She gazed at him sidelong. "Are you scandalized?"

"Not at all. I believe swimming to be a useful skill for men and women alike." His voice lowered. "Although I suppose the degree of scandal depends on what you and your sister were wearing to swim."

Had Mr. Darcy made an indelicate comment? For a moment she almost disbelieved her ears.

"With such beauty on display, I am certain it was a most arresting sight." As he continued, his eyes fell on her, leaving no doubt that he intended the suggestiveness.

Is he flirting with me? As her cheeks flushed, she resolved not to reveal that she bathed in the pond unclothed. "I wore a bathing costume at the beach."

"I see. It is a shame that men and women traditionally occupy different parts of the beach. I am sure you appear quite lovely in your bathing costume."

Unsure how to respond to such a statement, Elizabeth remained silent. *How did he change from angry to flirtatious so swiftly? And why?*

His eyes were half-closed but gazed only at her. *He wants me to know he still entertains romantic feelings for me.* This realization both thrilled and confused her.

Mr. Darcy continued. "If you have only just arrived in Brighton you may not have had an opportunity to visit the sights."

Elizabeth cleared her throat. "Not many, no."

"I have visited the town a few times. Perhaps I might escort you to some of the points of interest?"

She should say no. She should remain as far as possible from Mr. Darcy. But no doubt he would be a most engaging tour guide for the town; Mr. Wickham seemed best suited to recommend the best pubs. Despite his pride and disdain, Mr. Darcy would be a far more agreeable companion for a few hours of touring Brighton.

She should find some reason to refuse, but her mind could not find an acceptable excuse. He might take it as a sign that she preferred Mr. Wickham, and she did not want to leave him with that impression. She also owed the master of Pemberley an apology. "That would be most agreeable," she said finally.

"Excellent." Mr. Darcy smiled. "Could I call on you soon at the colonel's house?"

"Of course," she said faintly. *What have I done?*

"Very good." With a nod of his head, Mr. Darcy swept her back into the dance, and they spoke little.

Chapter Six

Elizabeth sat in Colonel Forster's drawing room, her eyes focused on her embroidery while her mind was not. They had been in Brighton for six days, and she had made almost no progress in uncovering Mr. Wickham's nefarious plans.

She had not expected to find a manuscript labeled "My Plans for Betraying England," but she had hoped for some clues about how he was accessing secret information or the location of the spies' hideout.

However, Mr. Wickham seemed perfectly at ease and was rarely absent on mysterious errands. Elizabeth had relayed the names of his friends to Colonel Forster, who had found little reason to be concerned about them. If only Mr. Wickham had introduced her to a suspicious French émigré with mysterious sources of income! Then the entire business might be on a path to conclusion.

Colonel Forster was not impatient with her but apparently had made little progress with his own investigations. More than once he shrugged and told Elizabeth that sometimes the game of espionage was played at a leisurely pace.

Today Mr. Wickham had promised to pay a call, and Elizabeth was determined to elicit information from him. Fortunately, the colonel had sent Lydia on a shopping expedition with his wife, so her sister would not be glaring jealous daggers at her when the officer visited.

Already Elizabeth had been waiting an hour, constantly sticking herself with the needle when her attention wandered from her embroidery. Finally, a knock sounded at the front door. However, when the housekeeper opened the drawing room door, she announced, "Mr. Darcy to see you, miss."

Oh heavens, what should I do now? At the ball a few days ago, Mr. Darcy had promised to call upon her, but when he had not, she had been relieved. If Elizabeth took a walk or a drive with him now, she would miss Mr. Wickham's arrival. But if Mr. Darcy remained, it would create an awkward scene when the other man arrived. Was there some way she could induce Mr. Darcy to depart? She could think of nothing.

Elizabeth put aside her embroidery and rose. "Thank you, Dawkins. I am certain Colonel Forster would like to see Mr. Darcy as well." At least she could avoid being alone with him. Dawkins escorted the man into the room and exited, closing the door behind her.

"I pray you have a seat, Mr. Darcy." She gestured to a chair across the room, but he took the one closest to her settee, perching on the edge of the chair with his hat resting on his knee. She managed not to sigh; apparently, he was determined to be difficult. "It is so good of you to call."

He cleared his throat. "I, er, said I would. I apologize for not arriving sooner. I was obliged to return to London for business."

"Of course. You are forgiven," she said lightly.

Mr. Darcy frowned as if he would have preferred not to be forgiven. "And I brought you a gift."

Elizabeth tilted her head inquisitively. He appeared to have nothing on his person.

Before she said anything, the door burst open, and Dawkins bustled in, carrying the most magnificent display of hothouse flowers Elizabeth had ever seen. Why there must have been a dozen or more roses, both pink and red, plus a profusion of other blossoms whose names Elizabeth did not know. She could not suppress a gasp.

"Here you go, miss," the housekeeper announced in a voice full of admiration for the gift. "I took the liberty of putting them in a vase for you." She set a crystal vase exploding with riotous color on the table beside Elizabeth's settee before hurrying out again.

She was quite overwhelmed by their magnificence—as well as the wealth on display. She could not imagine what they had cost. "I am—I thank you. They are lovely."

He inclined his head in acknowledgement.

The flowers were so beautiful she could scarcely look away from them. "I hardly know what to say."

At least this dispels any doubts about whether he intends to court me, she thought with dismay, ignoring the secret thrill that raced down her spine. No man would buy such a bouquet to express friendship. In fact, they constituted a gauntlet thrown at Mr. Wickham's feet—a declaration of intentions. Mr. Darcy knew the officer could not match such an extravagant gift; perhaps he hoped the other man would see them in the colonel's drawing room.

Elizabeth smiled inwardly at the thought of the officer's dismay. *Wait! I do not want Mr. Wickham to be unhappy. I cannot encourage Mr. Darcy.* Why was that simple fact so difficult to remember?

Mr. Darcy regarded her with his peculiar intensity. "Say you will accompany me on a ride about town. I have a curricle with a fine set of matched bays, and the weather is magnificent."

The idea was quite tempting, but surely she could not accept for Mr. Wickham's sake. Elizabeth opened her mouth to decline, but no sound emerged. Colonel Forster's entrance saved her from the necessity of an immediate response. The two men exchanged handshakes and pleasantries. They knew each other from Meryton, of course, but she did not believe their acquaintance was extensive. Dawkins soon followed with a tea service, which Elizabeth poured.

"What brings you to Brighton?" the colonel asked Mr. Darcy when they had all been served. Elizabeth peered up from her cup, curious about the response. "Do you have some business here?"

Mr. Darcy's eyes were fixed on his tea. "Not as such, no." He hesitated a moment. "I enjoy the seaside and thought to visit before the weather turns cold."

By himself? Certainly wealthy men could indulge their whims, but Mr. Darcy hardly seemed the sort of man who would impulsively travel across the country simply for some pleasant scenery.

"Did you ride all the way from Derbyshire?" the colonel asked. "It must have taken days."

Mr. Darcy rested a biscuit on the edge of his saucer. "Not so far. I was in Hertfordshire."

"Hertfordshire?" The word burst from Elizabeth before she could stop it. Why had he been in that part of the country?

"Yes…um…" Mr. Darcy colored and fixed his attention on the biscuit. "I…ah…was visiting Netherfield with Bingley. I thought you might have received news of it."

Mr. Bingley! "No," Elizabeth said faintly. "I have not received a letter for a couple of days." *I must write to Jane! How had such a visit come about? Had Jane seen Mr. Bingley?* Elizabeth bubbled over with questions. "Mr. Bingley remained in Hertfordshire?"

"Yes." Mr. Darcy cleared his throat. "I believe he has some plans for improvements to Netherfield."

"He is not planning to give it up?" This was the best news Elizabeth had received in weeks.

"I do not believe so." Mr. Darcy colored slightly. Was he recalling their conversation about Mr. Bingley at Hunsford? Had he played a role in his friend's return to Netherfield?

The colonel scrutinized Mr. Darcy carefully. "And you decided to follow my regiment to Brighton? Are you so desperate for fellow whist players?"

Mr. Darcy chuckled good-naturedly. "No…um…Rather you might say I was inspired by news of your departure. It occurred to me that now would be an ideal season for visiting Brighton." Glancing up, he caught and held Elizabeth's eyes for several seconds before looking away.

It was impossible to mistake his meaning. Elizabeth felt faint. *He came to Brighton for me! He had visited Longbourn, discovered I was in Brighton with Mr. Wickham, and traveled here—alone and on horseback—because he feared for my safety…*

As warmth flooded her heart, any residual irritation melted away. The man might be proud and high-handed, but she could not remain indifferent to these signs of his concern. If only there were some way she could reassure him that she was not under Mr. Wickham's spell! He did not deserve to labor under such a delusion.

"I just invited Miss Elizabeth for a drive in my curricle," Mr. Darcy informed the colonel. "I guessed that—since you have not been in Brighton long—she has not seen much of the town or surrounding countryside?"

Oh yes! At that moment Elizabeth wanted nothing more than an afternoon in Mr. Darcy's company. He had set aside any grievances and any resentment for the sake of her safety. No one, not even members of her family, had ever shown such concern for her. *I will give him my afternoon. I will laugh at his jokes. I will let him kiss me if he asks.* Although the thought was shocking, she found herself staring at his lips and wondering how they would feel pressed against hers.

The colonel cleared his throat, drawing Elizabeth's attention with a stern expression. Naturally he did not find Mr. Darcy so charming; instead, he was concerned about the man's effect on her mission. Reality crashed into her fantasy. *I have a mission. I must remain in the house to await Mr. Wickham's visit.* "Miss Bennet has a previous engagement with Mr. Wickham," the colonel informed Mr. Darcy frostily.

If only she could wipe away the crestfallen expression on Mr. Darcy's face! "Not so much an engagement," she clarified. "He merely said he might call…"

Dawkins appeared in the doorway. "Mr. Wickham, miss."

Elizabeth suppressed an urge to sigh. The timing could not be more unfortunate. Mr. Wickham ambled into the room on the housekeeper's heels and greeted the colonel. "Miss Elizabeth," he then crooned, taking her hand and kissing it far longer than was proper. Straightening, he gave Mr. Darcy a baleful look. "Darcy."

"Wickham." The other man's head barely moved.

The militia officer settled into the sofa, projecting ease and confidence. "I must beg your forgiveness for my tardiness. Just as I was preparing to depart the barracks, the lieutenant saw fit to send me on an errand."

"Of course." Elizabeth's mind worked frantically, trying to find a way to smooth the awkwardness. *I must fulfill my mission for the colonel, but Mr. Darcy...*

When had Mr. Darcy's happiness become such an important consideration to her?

Oblivious to Elizabeth's consternation, Mr. Wickham gave her a lazy grin. "I have rented a rig for the day; the weather is lovely. I thought we might drive along the cliffs. Denny said the view is magnificent." As his eyes ranged over the drawing room, they rested for a brief, triumphant moment on his rival.

Mr. Darcy leaned forward in his chair. "Miss Elizabeth will accompany *me* on a drive. I have already invited her."

The colonel cleared his throat. "Mr. Wickham said he would call today." Elizabeth did not blame Mr. Darcy for scowling; that hardly constituted a prior engagement.

Elizabeth gritted her teeth. Indeed, she would prefer to join Mr. Darcy, but she had not agreed to accompany him—and now he was speaking for her. He could be so high-handed!

Courtesy dictated that she should accept the first offer—Mr. Darcy's. However, Mr. Wickham was observing his rival with a curled lip; he would not take kindly to losing this contest. If he perceived that Elizabeth had jilted him, she might lose his favor.

Both men regarded Elizabeth with barely suppressed agitation, awaiting her decision. Her stomach twisted itself into a knot, reluctant to make the choice she knew she should.

Taking a deep breath, she turned to Mr. Darcy. "Perhaps you and I may take a drive another time?" His lips parted slightly as if he could only just restrain himself from gaping in astonishment. Did the man believe he was irresistible? Then an expression of great pain drifted over his face— to be replaced almost immediately with a polite, distant expression. This mask slid into place so quickly Elizabeth was not certain she had glimpsed anything else.

"Mr. Wickham incurred the expense of hiring a rig," she explained, projecting a gaiety she did not experience. "His efforts should not be in vain."

Mr. Darcy gave a stiff nod. "Of course. Tomorrow, perhaps, if the weather continues fine?"

Why was the prospect so tempting? *Mr. Darcy is often stiff and unpleasant*, she reminded herself. Yet her heart leapt at the thought of a drive with him; perhaps it was simply that any man would be an improvement over Mr. Wickham. "Of course—if the weather is fine."

"I await your pleasure." His gaze met hers with such intensity that she feared she might burst into flames. *Oh my*.

She knew not how long they stared at each other, but finally Mr. Wickham cleared his throat rather forcefully, and the spell was broken. Mr. Darcy stood, placed his hat on his head, and nodded to everyone in the room. "Until tomorrow, then."

Elizabeth sighed with relief when the door closed behind him.

***

Stepping onto the street, Darcy reassured himself that he only *felt* as if Elizabeth had stabbed him in the chest and torn a jagged rip in his heart. His chest ached as if she had, but any wounds were symbolic. *Get a hold of yourself, Darcy. You are being overly dramatic.*

He walked unsteadily toward his curricle, untied the horses, climbed in, and took the reins to set the carriage in motion, unconcerned about the direction. Georgiana teased him about being too dour: "Always search for the bright side, Will." Was there a bright side despite Elizabeth's rejection? Was there some glimmer of hope? Darcy's mind worked furiously to find one. *She did not accept a proposal of marriage from Wickham. He did not declare his undying love. They did not kiss.*

"Bah!" Darcy chastised himself. "I am grasping at straws." Elizabeth might not have declared her devotion to Wickham, but her decision was tantamount to it. Darcy had arrived first. Darcy had been the first to offer an outing. Darcy had had the stable hands polish the carriage and brush the horses until they shone. As he had staggered from the colonel's house, Darcy had spied the rig Wickham had rented; such paltry nags could not compare to Darcy's matched bays.

But none of these considerations had swayed Elizabeth.

His hands squeezed the reins until his knuckles turned white. The obvious reason was that she truly loved Wickham. Darcy found this difficult to accept, but perhaps his own wishful thinking prevented him from perceiving her dispassionately.

I have so much to offer her! Darcy could not help recalling all the women he had encountered through the years—beautiful, accomplished ladies who wore the latest fashions and the finest jewels. Not one of them made his heart race as Elizabeth did. Her smile, her wit, her conversation… He had never known a woman who was her equal. It did not signify that she lacked the latest fashions or the finest jewels…or the matched bays.

"Damnation!" His exclamation was loud enough that a few heads turned on the street. If she truly loved Wickham, Darcy could not change that. He could offer his carriage, his home, his name, his hand on bended knee—and nothing would sway her. Inconstancy was not in her nature. Many women would forsake a poor suitor for a man of greater fortune, but Elizabeth was not such a woman—or she would not be a woman Darcy could love.

But why was she so constant to Wickham?

To Darcy's—admittedly biased—eye she did not appear particularly besotted with Wickham, and the idea of a drive with Darcy appeared to tempt her. Yet she had most definitely chosen Wickham.

What I need is a good stiff drink or two…or three. His rig had been wandering the streets of Brighton aimlessly; miraculously he had not completely lost his bearings. Now he scrutinized his surroundings. By chance he was not too far from his lodgings, but he would find no libations there. Unfortunately, he had not thought to bring brandy during his frantic race to the coast.

Ah…yes! There was a pub: the Three Ships. It appeared reputable enough, and at this time of day it would be sparsely populated. Darcy could enjoy a table to himself.

When he appeared in the doorway, the barkeeper hurried up to him and inquired as to his pleasure. The establishment likely did not see many men dressed in so fine a fashion. However, Darcy was in no mood for company, obsequious or otherwise. He merely requested a private table.

The pub was relatively clean, and he was the only patron. The barkeeper sat him beside a window, with glass that was rippled and distorted but covered in only a superficial layer of grime. The table itself was pitted and scarred and showed the remnants of spilled ale and past meals, but Darcy had visited worse pubs.

A barmaid bustled over. Quite a bit older than most in her profession, she was buxom and matronly with a broad smile on her face. "Och!" she exclaimed immediately. "What did she do to you, lad?"

"I beg your pardon?" Darcy asked. Nobody had addressed him as "lad" for quite some time.

"She broke your heart, didn't she?"

Darcy was unsure whether he was more startled by the woman's effrontery or her perspicacity. Usually he was loath to discuss his private concerns with anyone, particularly strangers, but for some reason the idea held some appeal at this moment. Perhaps it was the sympathetic tilt to her head. Perhaps it was simply that he had no one else with whom he could discuss them.

"I suppose she did," Darcy answered slowly.

The barmaid shook her head slowly. "Tell Peg about it. Did she go and marry another fellow?"

Darcy's hands clenched involuntarily. "Not…yet."

"Then there's still hope!"

"I do not believe so." His heart ached at the admission.

The woman stuck her hands deep into the pockets of her skirt. "And why would that be?'

"She chose to take a carriage ride with him today. He is a thoroughgoing blackguard, and she knows it and yet…"

"Hmm." The barmaid tapped her lip thoughtfully. "Have you asked her about him?"

Of course, he had! This was a waste of time, but out of politeness Darcy answered, "Yes, but she told me almost nothing."

"She knows he's a scoundrel?"

"Yes!" Darcy suppressed a desire to tell her everything. "I had thought her of better discernment than that."

"Did you talk with her when there is nobody around to hear you?"

Darcy rolled his eyes. "No. It would not be appropriate to be alone with her—"

She waved this objection away. "Psh! Folks of quality have such strange ideas! Appropriate? Who would care?"

"Her father, for one."

"Very well, but—" Peg slipped into the chair opposite Darcy's and lowered her voice. Her presumption should have offended Darcy, but he found it rather amusing. "Perhaps you might get a few moments alone with her on a walk or at a dinner. Give her a chance to tell you the whole story."

Darcy sighed, tracing one of the grooves in the table with his finger. "I fear that the whole story is that she is in love with the scoundrel."

"Did she tell you that?" Darcy shook his head. "Why would she love him if he is a blackguard?"

"In my experience, love rarely makes sense." Darcy himself was proof of that.

"But she's a sensible, clever woman?"

"Yes."

"Perhaps there is another reason for her behavior."

Darcy frowned, unsure what Peg meant. "Such as..."

The barmaid shrugged expressively. "I don't know, do I? But my niece Becky once was in a fix. Her papa told her to be nice to a fellow she didn't much like. He was courting her, and she had to smile and dance with him and pretend as though she enjoyed it."

Darcy leaned forward, intrigued despite himself. "Why?"

The woman's hands fluttered. "Oh, her papa owed the fellow some money, and Becky is a pretty thing. The man said he'd forgive the papa's debts if she married him. Becky continued for months being friendly to this man when she couldn't stand the sight of him—until finally she ran off with a fisherman."

Darcy slumped back in his chair, staring at Peg, aware that his mouth was hanging open. He had never considered the possibility that Wickham exerted some sort of hold over Elizabeth.

Did Mr. Bennet owe money to Wickham? Unlikely. But there were many other reasons Elizabeth might be compelled to show friendliness to the officer. Half a dozen ideas occurred to Darcy immediately. Perhaps—fearing an elopement—she sought to distract Wickham's attention from Lydia. Perhaps Wickham knew something damning about a member of the Bennet family and was blackmailing her. Perhaps he held some other monetary inducement over her head. As Darcy well knew, Wickham was capable of any number of unsavory schemes.

Elizabeth could be desperately in need of Darcy's assistance, not his condemnation.

Peg waggled her finger in his face, chuckling at his no-doubt stunned expression. "See, you hadn't thought of that, had you?"

"No," Darcy admitted. He could easily resolve most difficulties with money. Elizabeth could indeed be suffering without such resources.

Peg gave a decisive nod of her head. "That's why you need to speak to the young woman—alone."

Darcy could only nod mutely. Why had this not occurred to him before?

The woman stood with a grin. "Now, what can I get you to drink?" Suddenly getting foxed had no appeal.

"I must depart." Darcy reached into his pocket and pulled out a coin. It was far more than he would pay for a whisky, but no matter. "I thank you for your excellent counsel." After dropping the coin into her palm, he hurried from the pub. There was no time to waste.

Chapter Seven

Elizabeth Bennet had enjoyed many carriage rides in her life. This was not one of them. Mr. Wickham drove too fast and too recklessly, no doubt under the mistaken impression that swaggering would impress her. Instead, she clutched the edge of her seat with one hand and her bonnet with the other while forcing a grin as though she were having the time of her life. Occasionally she stifled a desire to scream for him to stop the curricle so she could climb down and walk back to the colonel's house.

This was not the sort of danger she anticipated when agreeing to become a spy. One boon of the ride was that fear for her life occupied her thoughts so completely that she stopped thinking about her regrets over rejecting Mr. Darcy. She feared she had hurt him badly.

Elizabeth earned a temporary reprieve from the anxiety-inducing drive when they reached the cliffside road. Declaring that she wished to walk along the clifftops for a better view, she insisted that Mr. Wickham stop the carriage. Indeed, it was a lovely sight; the stark whitish gray cliffs contrasted against the luminous blue of the sky. Golden sunlight sparkled through many layers of ocean water. Seabirds whirled and dove through the air. Grasses on the top of the cliffs rippled in the wind.

At the colonel's house, Mr. Wickham suggested that Mr. Denny had told him about the cliffside walk, but it quickly became clear that he was quite familiar with the area. After a few minutes on solid ground, Elizabeth's heart had stopped thundering in her chest, and she proceeded to calculate how she could pry some information out of Mr. Wickham. The colonel was particularly interested in discovering where Wickham met with his French compatriots; most likely it was in one of the caves that lined the cliffs.

She peered down at the craggy, white chalk cliffs. "Is it true that there are caves along these cliffs?"

Wickham had one booted foot propped against a boulder, no doubt believing he made a very dashing picture. "Caves? Aye, hundreds I have heard."

"Really?" Elizabeth opened her mouth in a perfect "o." "Do you suppose any of them are used by *smugglers*?"

Wickham adjusted his hat to a slightly jaunty angle. "No doubt they are. There are smugglers all over this part of the country."

Imagining how Lydia would react, Elizabeth gasped. "Do you think so?"

He smirked at her innocence. "I *know* so. The navy patrols the Channel, but there are too many smugglers to catch them all."

She gave a little excited shiver. "And they could be using the caves right here—beneath our feet?"

"I suppose. Although most of the caves are small and shallow. They would not be of much use to smugglers."

"But surely there are *some* which are used by smugglers?" Elizabeth shuffled closer to the edge, peering downward. She casually grasped Wickham's forearm to steady herself and heard him hiss in response. Good. His attraction to her might help cloud his judgment. "Do *you* know of any real smugglers' caves?"

Mr. Wickham paused, clearly torn between the need for secrecy and the desire to impress a young woman.

She allowed excitement to show on her face. "You do! I can tell. I would love to visit a smugglers' cave! It would be like a scene in a novel!"

"I do know the location of a few caves," he conceded.

"Would you take me to see one? Please!"

"The climb down is long and dangerous."

"I do not mind. I like a long climb. It will be an adventure!" How could she overcome his reluctance? "Oh, I can just imagine it!" She pitched her voice lower, more enticing. "You and me...alone in a cave..."

Mr. Wickham swallowed hard before seizing her hand. "Very well, I will take you to the cave. But I did warn you about the climb."

The path down to the beach was indeed steep. Although she had worn her sturdiest half boots, Elizabeth's feet slid on the loose dirt more than once. Mr. Wickham held her hand, and she did not fall.

The beach was narrow and completely deserted, too rocky and inaccessible for casual visitors. Waves crashed onto the shore with magnificent sprays of water—far more ferocious than at the ladies' beach. If only she could stay and admire the sight; under other circumstances and with different company she would have loved to linger. But Mr. Wickham was already tugging impatiently at her hand.

They tramped along the beach for several minutes until they came to the cave—its entrance almost completely concealed by a large boulder. Elizabeth had to turn sideways and squeeze between the boulder and the cliff face to enter, but the interior was surprisingly large and dry, with a sandy floor and craggy stone walls. Surveying the space, Elizabeth focused on memorizing the details of the location—only belatedly realizing she should be "impressed" with her companion's cleverness.

"Oh my!" she exclaimed, putting a hand to her mouth and imagining how Lydia would react. "This is a *real* cave. I do not believe I have ever encountered a real cave before! How thrilling!" Wickham preened. "It is ever so much larger than I thought it could be," she warbled as she explored the space, hoping to find useful clues for the colonel. Deeper into the cliff, the cave narrowed and disappeared into darkness. "What is back there?" She gestured.

"I don't know. Perhaps others have explored it, but I have not," Mr. Wickham responded.

Elizabeth's shiver was not entirely feigned. "Perhaps there is a secret passageway."

The officer smirked. "Perhaps."

Finding nothing else of note in the back of the cave, she returned to the cave's mouth. Unfortunately, this also brought her into greater proximity to Mr. Wickham. When enticing him, Elizabeth had weighed the danger that the scoundrel might make improper advances. She did not believe he would try to force her while she was under the colonel's protection, but still…

As he drew closer, she whirled away, searching for some distraction. She pointed to a pile of crates stacked against the cave wall. "What is the purpose of those?"

"Don't touch them!" he said with a hint of panic in his voice. "Who knows what the smugglers might do if we disturb their wares." Hmm. That would definitely be of interest to the colonel.

Elizabeth giggled as if thrilled by this thought. "Have you ever *seen* the smugglers? How do they appear? Are they at all like pirates?"

"No. They're a rather rough lot."

She faked a shiver of fear. "They could arrive at any moment. Perhaps we should leave!"

Mr. Wickham chuckled. "I believe they mainly work at night."

"Oh."

The officer was close to her—far closer than was appropriate. Before she could duck away, his lips were on hers. Suppressing her natural revulsion, she drew upon every ounce of thespian skill to act the part of the besotted lover. The man did not make it easy. His lips were dry, the stubble of his beard scratched her chin, and his breath stank of gin.

She attempted to return his kisses with equal ardor but found that attraction was difficult to feign in such close proximity. Mr. Darcy would be more pleasant to kiss. His lips looked quite soft, and he would no doubt hold her gently and lovingly—not roughly as if he wanted to possess her. Indeed, kissing Mr. Darcy would not be a hardship.

The man she kissed moaned, and Elizabeth was jarringly reminded that he was not Mr. Darcy.

Why am I thinking of Mr. Darcy now? Why am I thinking of him at all?

Lost in fantasies about the master of Pemberley, she had apparently returned Mr. Wickham's kisses rather enthusiastically. His tongue was in her mouth! His hands had wandered up her legs and over her thighs to her waist—and threatened to travel higher. This needed to stop immediately.

Pulling her mouth from his, she said, "Mr. Wickham, perhaps we should—"

He continued to trail kisses along her shoulder. "Elizabeth, don't you love me?"

"Of course, I do."

He regarded her with a soft, wounded expression. "It is only a matter of time until we are married—until I have the funds to marry. What does it matter if we anticipate the vows?"

How many women had succumbed to such promises from Mr. Wickham? He was so very practiced in the art of seduction. Elizabeth refused to be his victim. *But I must deter him without giving the least suspicion of the disgust he provokes in me.*

Mistaking her silence for assent, Mr. Wickham pulled her closer as his hands ranged up her body from her waist to her—

"What is that sound?" she asked suddenly, pushing him away and allowing her very real anxiety at the situation to color her voice.

"What sound?" The man continued to nibble her neck. It tickled, but perhaps some women liked the sensation.

She pushed him away more forcefully. "I heard voices and footsteps! The smugglers are returning!"

The officer cocked his head to one side and listened. "I hear nothing."

She shook her head frantically. "The sound of the waves has swallowed it up again. But I tell you, the smugglers are coming!" She scrambled for purchase in the sand as she hurried for the exit.

"There's no cause for worry..." Mr. Wickham reached for her.

She paused and stiffened in her tracks. "The sound comes again!"

"I heard nothing—"

She lowered her voice to a whisper. "My family always said my hearing was exceptionally acute."

For the first time his face betrayed anxiety as his eyebrows shot upward. "They did?"

She edged closer to the cave entrance; Mr. Wickham would not try anything improper on a public beach. "We must leave now before they arrive—or we will be trapped here! They will slit our throats! They will pillage and burn our houses to the ground!"

"I still hear nothing." Mr. Wickham's tone was very exasperated as he touched her arm.

"Just the thought gives me such anxiety—such tremblings and flutterings in my heart—oh, my nerves! My nerves cannot withstand it!" Barely evading his hand, she raced to the cave entrance. *Let him think me a silly female, scared of nothing and allowing my imagination to run wild. At least I will be a silly female with my virtue intact.*

As she squeezed herself through the entrance, Mr. Wickham made a frustrated noise and muttered curses under his breath, but he followed her from the cave.

Once on the beach, Elizabeth raced toward the path that had brought them from the cliff top. Outside the cave, the absence of smugglers would be obvious, and Elizabeth had no desire to discuss it with her companion.

"Elizabeth!" he yelled. "Nobody else is here!"

"They must be in hiding!" she cried over her shoulder, not slowing her pace. "Smugglers are most clever!" It was not necessary that he believe in the existence of the smugglers, only that she believed in them. "We cannot remain. Not one minute more!" Lifting her skirts to her knees, she increased her speed. Perhaps the sight of her legs would distract Mr. Wickham from the absent smugglers. Within minutes she arrived at the base of the cliff pathway. There she paused, not relishing the thought of climbing without a steadying hand.

Unencumbered by skirts, Mr. Wickham reached the path only moments later. Panting hard, he scowled at her. "Stupid girl!" he chastised. "No one was there, and there was no reason to panic."

If Elizabeth had been in love with the officer, his disdainful tone would have crushed her spirit. Although it would have made it easier to overcome any infatuation with him. Loving a man like Mr. Wickham would probably make her forswear love for the rest of her life. Thank God her heart was safe from him! As it was, his derogatory comments merely heightened her contempt for him.

"I have had enough of caves." She tossed her head as Lydia might. "Will you assist me in ascending the pathway, Mr. Wickham? Or shall I struggle to climb it alone?"

With a sour expression, the man offered Elizabeth his hand as he climbed onto the pathway. She sighed with relief; apparently, he had forsaken all plans for seduction.

She had discovered his secret cave and emerged unscathed. The day was a success.

***

The moment the door closed behind Elizabeth, a great weight lifted from her shoulders. Safe within Colonel Forster's house, she could anticipate a few delightful hours free of Mr. Wickham and the need to dissemble. Immediately, she knocked on the door to the colonel's study and was admitted. The colonel was thrilled by her news about the cave and showed her a map of the coastline so she might pinpoint the location. "This is excellent information, Miss Elizabeth! Quite excellent. I had been dubious whether a woman could be of any service in this endeavor, but you are a credit to your sex."

Elizabeth bristled. "I would imagine that the army might find women of great usefulness as spies if they deigned to employ them."

"Indeed." The colonel laughed. Elizabeth did not join him since she had not made a joke. She stood, intending to depart.

The colonel held up a hand, and she sank into her chair again. "I had another matter to discuss with you. How well-acquainted are you with Mr. Darcy?"

Elizabeth's stomach plummeted. Did he suspect some sort of inappropriate attachment? Although she made great effort not to display any particular interest in the master of Pemberley, no one could deny that he was pursuing her. Had the colonel noticed her unease in the man's presence? Would she be forced to reveal the proposal at Hunsford? She did not believe she was equal to describing such a mortifying scene.

"N-Not terribly well," she stammered. "We conversed a few times in Hertfordshire, and I encountered him again at his aunt's estate in Kent."

"It is rather convenient that he appeared at the same time as Mr. Wickham—without a plausible reason for the journey."

Elizabeth wanted to laugh, although she did not know whether from relief or exasperation. "You think Mr. Darcy could be conspiring with Mr. Wickham?"

"Wickham claims to know the man since childhood. It would be easy for him to draw Darcy into his plots—or vice versa. Darcy certainly has the fortune to fund such an endeavor."

Elizabeth stifled a smile and tried to respond rationally. "I thought you were seeking a co-conspirator who was privy to sensitive military information. Mr. Darcy would hardly be that."

The colonel dismissed her objection with a negligent wave of his hand that Elizabeth found infuriating. "Perhaps there is yet a third person," he said. "Or perhaps Wickham himself has somehow been gaining access to my private papers."

How could she convey the absurdity of his supposition about Mr. Darcy without revealing the truth? "Mr. Wickham and Mr. Darcy dislike each other," she insisted. "They never exchanged words in Meryton—only sneers."

"Perhaps. Or their mutual antipathy could be an elaborate ruse. I find it curious that the man was so eager to call upon my home; perhaps he was seeking information."

Oh, this is frustrating! I know why Mr. Darcy arrived so suddenly in Brighton. He is concerned for me; he does not want me keeping company with Mr. Wickham. However, she could not convince the colonel of this truth without sharing their entire history. Elizabeth had not even informed her father of Mr. Darcy's proposal; she could hardly tell the colonel first.

Her fingernails bit into her palms. "Mr. Darcy would never betray his country!" she insisted. "He would find the very idea repugnant." Even as the words emerged from her mouth, Elizabeth wondered at herself. *Why do I care so deeply for Mr. Darcy's reputation?* Surely the colonel's opinion will have little effect on the man's life, but she could not shake her anger at the injustice of the accusation. She could only point to the most obvious conclusion. "He visited your home because he wishes to court me."

The colonel regarded her steadily for a moment and then sank back into his chair. "Does he? I find that curious as well. You are without fortune or name of consequence. You are pretty enough, I grant you, but why would he take the time for a courtship? The master of Pemberley would not marry a country miss."

By now the blood was boiling in Elizabeth's veins, and she was compelled to cover her mouth with a hand lest she blurt out the truth: that Mr. Darcy had made her an offer previously.

She managed to bite her tongue, but the colonel's character was sinking rapidly in her estimation.

Oblivious to the reactions of the woman before him, the colonel continued. "He may simply be dallying with you. Wealthy men are often prone to licentious behavior." He dismissed the potential damage to Elizabeth's heart with a shrug. "Just guard your tongue in his presence; he might repeat your words to Wickham. And be sure to report anything suspicious he says."

Elizabeth restrained an urge to roll her eyes. "I will take all due precautions," she promised, with no intention of spying on Mr. Darcy or any expectations he would do anything to warrant particular scrutiny.

She blew out a breath, trying to quell her irritation. Mr. Darcy was an honorable man, proud of his family name, and should not be subject to such unfounded suspicions.

"Very good." The colonel nodded once and bent his head to the papers on his desk. Dismissed, Elizabeth stood and stalked from the room with quick jerky movements, stifling an impulse to slam the door.

I must simply get the necessary information from Mr. Wickham, and then this sorry business will be through and done. Elizabeth could not wait.

Chapter Eight

Darcy had been lurking outside Colonel Forster's house for at least an hour. He had varied his locations: a shadowy archway, the corner of the street, the alley opposite the home's door. He was not precisely hiding, just doing his best to be inconspicuous. Still, he worried that one of the colonel's more observant neighbors would suspect him of being a rather well-dressed footpad.

He shifted his weight to the other foot and leaned against the alley's brick wall. He needed to speak with Elizabeth alone, which would not happen if he knocked on the door of the colonel's house. Elizabeth loved to walk; surely she would venture out at some point.

At that moment the door opened, and Elizabeth emerged. Darcy held his breath, but luck was with him: she was alone. She set a brisk pace leading directly into the heart of Brighton. Perhaps she needed to do a little shopping. Well, that suited Darcy's plans as well.

He followed at a distance as she passed into the most fashionable part of the town, walking past the prince regent's Royal Pavilion. Rumors said the prince was in Brighton, but being naturally indolent, the man was unlikely to venture out into the town, which was just as well.

Now they were far enough from the colonel's house that she would not suspect him of following her. All this deception made his stomach ache, but he was compelled to follow the dictates of propriety—which definitely frowned upon the following of young women.

"Miss Bennet! Miss Bennet!" he called, hurrying up behind her just as she reached the edge of the Steyne. Originally a grassy area where local fishermen dried their nets, the Steyne was now more like a public park. The streets around it were touted as some of the most fashionable addresses in Brighton. Mrs. Fitzherbert, the prince regent's paramour, was known to keep a house overlooking the Steyne.

Today the green hosted some kind of market. Stalls of fruits, vegetables, and bread dotted the lawn, and the streets were crowded with people examining the wares.

Elizabeth turned at the sound of her name and noticed him with a lift of her eyebrows. "Mr. Darcy." Her tone was even. "I am visiting the market. Lydia's stomach is out of sorts, and I thought to find her a few apples—her favorite fruit."

"May I accompany you?"

Her hesitation twisted Darcy's heart. Did she still find his presence so distasteful? He straightened his shoulders and reminded himself that he was here to secure her safety. Her opinion of him was immaterial. "Of course," she said eventually.

However, she did not hesitate to take his arm, and they chatted about the weather as they ambled among the stalls in the market. She purchased three round, pink apples for her sister and placed them carefully in a basket resting over one arm. One vendor was selling an enticing array of biscuits, and Darcy bought lemon biscuits for them.

"This is delicious. Thank you!" Elizabeth said as she swallowed the last crumbs.

"My pleasure."

They had reached the end of the market stalls, but the green was dotted by benches. "Shall we sit?" Darcy asked, gesturing to a bench.

Again, Elizabeth hesitated. "I cannot linger for long." She sat on the bench indicated but positioned herself at the far end—clearly not inviting any intimacy.

Darcy occupied the other end, which was not very far on such a small bench. He stifled an impulse to take her hand; excessive familiarity now could only hurt his cause. He caught and held her eyes. "Miss Bennet, I must speak with you on a most serious matter."

Her mouth fell open, and he immediately realized she feared another proposal. He held up a hand, feeling suddenly ridiculous. "No, it is not that!" he said hastily. "First, I owe you an apology for my insulting behavior in Hunsford. When I recall my words about your family—"

Elizabeth raised her hand. "Speak no more on that subject. It is I who owe you an apology for my aspersions on your character. I shudder when I think of what I said then."

His lips twisted in a smile. "It seems each of us believes we are responsible for the greater portion of the blame."

She smiled as well. "Perhaps we may call it even and never mention the subject again."

Darcy's shoulders slumped with relief. "Agreed." Elizabeth gathered herself to stand, but he forestalled her with a gesture. "There is another subject I must discuss….It is about…Wickham."

Elizabeth pursed her lips. "I believe we have had this conversation."

"Yes, but I—" How could he address such a sensitive question? "I—It occurred to me that you—or your family—might be...in a difficult position regarding Mr. Wickham."

Her brows drew together as if his words mystified her.

"That you might be operating under some kind of duress...." Again, her face betrayed perplexity. Must he speak plainer about such an unsavory subject? "He has been known to threaten blackmail. And occasionally people owe him gambling debts..." He allowed his words to trail off suggestively.

Finally, realization dawned on her face. "Oh no! I thank you for your concern, but there is nothing of that nature concerning my family and Mr. Wickham."

Darcy believed her without reservation; her perplexity had been unfeigned. He was obscurely disappointed, realizing only then that he had envisioned himself as a rescuer who could solve her problems. "Why then?" he asked. "Why keep company with the man?" Desperation leaked into his voice. "Did you fail to read the letter I gave you?"

"I read every word," she said, not gazing in his direction.

Darcy's shoulders tightened. *She had? But—* "Did you not credit what I had written?"

"No. I believed it." She held herself quite stiff and still.

Worse and worse. She knew and believed Darcy's story about Wickham, but she chose to disregard it. A headache began to form at the base of his skull. "Then you know what the man is. Why do you maintain a friendship with him?"

Elizabeth's face had a determined, white-lipped expression that he remembered all too well from the Hunsford Parsonage. Apparently. he had a particular talent for provoking her anger. "I do not believe it is your business who I keep company with."

He chose his words carefully, having no desire to add fuel to the fire. "No, that is correct. However, I am concerned about you—as a friend. Wickham is a dangerous man."

Elizabeth gathered herself again, preparing to stand and leave him. "I am well able to protect myself."

Darcy stifled a groan. How many other women believed they were on their guard against the man's charms only to find themselves disgraced—or worse? "He possesses wiles and machinations that—"

She thrust to her feet. "That is enough, Mr. Darcy." Her voice was not loud, but firm. "You have discharged your duty by issuing your warning."

As she turned to leave, Darcy grabbed her hand desperately. "I pray you—do not accept a proposal of marriage from Wickham."

She did not immediately shake off his grip but stared down at him with an expression of shock, which soon turned into a tenderness that made Darcy's breath catch. "I promise you I will *never* accept an offer of marriage from that man."

He blew out a breath. Thank God! He still did not know why she was taking the scoundrel's part, but her promise suggested she had not been seduced by his charms. "I thank you, Miss Bennet. That eases my heart." He squeezed her hand in heartfelt gratitude.

"Elizabeth!" A male voice called from behind them.

Darcy swore silently; another minute alone with her and he might have succeeded in discovering her purpose. She jerked her hand out of Darcy's grasp as they both turned toward the source of the cry. Darcy stifled an oath at the sight of Wickham striding across the grass.

"Mr. Wickham!" Elizabeth cried with evident delight. She skipped in his direction and immediately linked arms with him. Darcy found it difficult to reconcile this unconstrained behavior with the thoughtful, reserved woman he had conversed with mere moments ago.

The officer greeted her with a sunny smile but glared at Darcy; perhaps he had noticed how their hands were linked. *Good*. "Darcy."

"Wickham."

"Mr. Darcy was kind enough to accompany me to the market," Elizabeth said stiffly, as if accepting his company was a painful duty she could not refuse. Did she really think it necessary to account for her actions to Wickham?

"I see," Wickham said with a curl of his lip.

"But I am very happy you have come!" Bouncing on her toes, she giggled. "Now we shall have the merriest time!" Had Darcy ever heard such a giggle issue from this woman? He should have been jealous that Wickham enjoyed these treasures; however, he now noticed signs of strain in her behavior. She was exerting effort to appear amiable in the man's company. He was only experiencing a false version of Elizabeth. But why? Why did she need to playact for the other man?

Apparently perceiving no falsity in her behavior, Wickham gave Darcy a self-satisfied grin. "Indeed, we shall. Would you like me to purchase you a biscuit?" He gestured toward the market.

Elizabeth clapped her hands together. "Oh yes, please!"

Wickham smirked as he nodded goodbye to Darcy and, with Elizabeth on his arm, turned toward the stalls.

Darcy's heart twisted itself into a knot as he observed the retreating figures—every step taking her farther from him. Yes, Darcy was now confident that Wickham did not command her heart. Nor did he wield power over her. Yet she accompanied him without hesitation—even with apparent joy. Despite her vow, Darcy's heart filled with misgivings. Perhaps Wickham *was* the one she wanted.

They had only traveled a few paces when Colonel Forster, striding purposefully from a side street, intercepted them. "Wickham! Miss Elizabeth!" His face was white and grave. "I have news of a most serious nature." Darcy stood and hastily joined the group; whatever the news, he must be available to assist and protect Elizabeth. The colonel spared him a brief, narrow-eyed glare before returning his attention to the others.

"What is it, sir?" Elizabeth asked. She and Wickham no longer linked arms, although they stood in closer proximity than Darcy would have liked.

The older man gripped Wickham's shoulder. "I am afraid there has been…a grim discovery. Denny. Robert Denny"—the colonel swallowed—"was discovered a few hours ago in a back alley near the beach. H-He is deceased."

"Oh!" Elizabeth cried as her hand flew to her mouth.

Wickham's mouth fell open. "What? What has happened?"

The colonel shook his head. "We are not certain, but it was not a natural death. I believe he was struck from behind with a heavy object."

Elizabeth gasped. "Murdered?"

"It appears so." The colonel's eyes were fixed on Wickham's face—evaluating the other man's reaction? "Since you were his particular friend, I wanted you to know immediately."

"Thank you, sir." The officer displayed the symptoms of horror and shock, but his hands were steady, and his face had not paled as the colonel's had. Was it possible Wickham already knew of Denny's demise?

"How horrible!" Elizabeth exclaimed.

"Indeed." The colonel addressed Wickham. "Were you aware of anyone who would wish to harm Denny?"

"No." Wickham scratched the back of his neck, looking at the green. "Everyone loved him."

"Well, we will learn the truth," the colonel vowed. "In the meantime, Miss Elizabeth, you should return to the house."

"But—" Elizabeth's gaze darted from the colonel to Wickham.

"You need time to recover from the shock." The colonel's tone was implacable.

"But surely Mr. Wickham will need his friends—"

"Mr. Wickham has friends in the militia." A touch of steel in his voice suggested that the colonel was issuing a command rather than a request. "Your sister and my wife are quite distraught. They would like some companionship."

Elizabeth started. "Oh yes, of course!"

"Wickham," the colonel said, "I will visit the barracks soon, and we will discuss this sad situation. Collect your fellow officers and retire there until I arrive."

Wickham saluted smartly and strode away.

"This is a sad business. Come away, Miss Bennet." With a slow shake of his head, the colonel held out his arm to Elizabeth. The man gave Darcy one more suspicious glare as he led her away. Elizabeth did not look at Darcy.

Long after they had disappeared from sight, Darcy stood on the grass and considered this grim news. He was certain Wickham had already known of his friend's death, and almost as certain that the colonel viewed the man with suspicion. Did he suspect Wickham of murdering his friend? Was it possible that Wickham *had* killed the man? The man was a scoundrel and a liar, but Darcy had not thought him as bad as all that.

It was as if he had a jigsaw puzzle composed entirely of pieces in the wrong shapes. His sole purpose had been saving Elizabeth from Wickham, but now he suspected he had stepped into the middle of something bigger and far more dangerous. Was Wickham associating with criminals? Smugglers? Highwaymen?

And how was Elizabeth involved? She was wrapped up in this mess. Did she know something of Wickham's sordid activities? How could Darcy protect her? After several seconds of indecision, Darcy strode away in the opposite direction.

***

The colonel walked with a fast and jerky stride; Elizabeth soon dropped his arm and simply tried to keep pace with his longer legs. Swinging at his side, his hands were clenched into fists, and a muscle worked in his jaw. He walked with a singleness of purpose, glancing neither left nor right. Several times she considered asking a question, but the expression on his face argued against it.

A man under his command was dead. Murdered. Naturally he was agitated. But he acted almost as if he were angry with Elizabeth, and she could not understand how she might have erred.

When they reached the colonel's residence, he held the door open for her and gestured for her to join him in the drawing room. While she seated herself on a settee, the colonel prowled about the room, apparently unable to rest. "We must discontinue your spy mission at once," he said without preamble. "I will return you and your sister to Hertfordshire on the first available coach."

Elizabeth blinked; she had not thought Mr. Denny's death might affect her mission. "But—"

He would not allow her to finish. "This mission has become far too dangerous. I will not put a young woman's life at risk."

She frowned. "You have no reason to believe Mr. Denny's death is related to Mr. Wickham or his espionage activities. He might have been killed in a barroom brawl."

The man stopped pacing for a moment. "I had not considered that possibility." Then he shook his head. "No, the risk is too great. Denny was a friend of Wickham's, and now he is dead. It is too great a coincidence."

"Surely you do not believe Mr. Wickham killed him! He seemed as surprised by the news as I was. If he were the man responsible, he is the best actor I have ever seen." Still, a little doubt niggled in the back of Elizabeth's mind. Mr. Wickham was an accomplished spinner of falsehoods; she herself had swallowed his lies readily enough.

The colonel sighed. "I do not know what to think. He did appear shocked, but I expected more grief."

"I believe it is unlikely that Mr. Wickham killed his friend, thus there is no increase in danger."

"No, it is too great a risk. I must return you to your home."

Elizabeth took a deep breath, trying to quell her rising agitation. The colonel had revealed the overbearing, stubborn side of his nature before, but never had so much been at stake.

For once in her life she was doing something important—work that would help her country—and she was expected to forsake the opportunity at the first sign of possible danger. It was unfair. "I am making progress with Mr. Wickham," she said. "Surely it cannot be too dangerous for me to stay two or three more days."

There was a long silence while the colonel considered. Finally, he sat heavily in an armchair. "You have been of immense assistance. Agents have located his hideout, and my men are observing the friends he mentioned to you." He ran a shaking hand through his hair. "Who knows what else the man might tell you? I would be loath to lose your help."

Elizabeth pressed her advantage. "If I leave now, Wickham's plans might succeed—and that could be disastrous for England." The colonel's expression suggested he was wavering. "Please let me stay. I will not hold you responsible for anything that happens. But I want to be of service to my country. Surely you can understand such a desire."

The colonel's shoulders sagged, and she tasted victory. "Very well, but you must exercise even greater caution."

"I will."

"If anything else untoward occurs, I will send you home immediately."

"I understand."

"Very well. I pray you venture upstairs now to comfort Miss Lydia and my wife. They were most distraught at the news about Mr. Denny. Wickham will be at his leisure later in the day. Perhaps you might learn more from him then." The colonel nodded a curt goodbye to her, turned on his heel, and left the room.

Elizabeth sagged against the back of the settee and wondered if it was possible to wring information from Mr. Wickham more quickly.

Chapter Nine

As he strode back to his lodgings, Darcy struggled to recall everything he could about Mr. Denny. He had a passing familiarity with the man, having conversed with him at a few events in Hertfordshire. The man had been pleasant enough, but he had also struck up a friendship with Wickham—which called into question not only his judgment but also his morals. Perhaps Denny was just as dissolute as Wickham and had been killed over gambling debts or meddling with some shopkeeper's daughter.

A prickle of unease ran down Darcy's spine. Wickham's friend was dead, and Elizabeth was all too friendly with Wickham. Whether or not Wickham had killed the man, Elizabeth could be in danger. Darcy shoved away the memory of the moment when Elizabeth had expressed a preference—once again—for Wickham's company over his. It was irrelevant now.

Obviously, he was missing several pieces of the puzzle, which was revealed to be far larger than he had initially understood. Or was he simply fooling himself? *Perhaps I want to believe Wickham is involved in nefarious activities to excuse Elizabeth's behavior. Perhaps she simply prefers Wickham to me.* Darcy's chest ached, and breathing became more difficult. No, someone killed Denny; there are larger forces at work here.

The Crescent was the first crescent building in Brighton and still considered the most fashionable. Darcy particularly enjoyed the seaside view, although he had passed scant time in his lodgings. At least his rooms offered solitude and quiet where he could ruminate on this situation and how he should address it.

Darcy had taken only a single step inside his rooms when Snell, his housekeeper, bustled up to him. He suppressed a sigh. A local woman, Snell was lonely and garrulous, but Darcy was not in the mood for inane conversation. However, she unexpectedly came to the point immediately. "You have a gentleman waiting for you in the drawing room."

Wonderful. Someone else to test the limits of Darcy's politeness before he could enjoy his solitude. But when Darcy entered the drawing room, the face that greeted him was as welcome as it was unforeseen. "Richard!"

His cousin, Colonel Richard Fitzwilliam, stood, giving Darcy a hearty handshake and a slap on the back. "What brings you to Brighton?"

Darcy asked. He had written to his cousin with his temporary address, but the return letter had given no hint that Richard might visit.

Richard's amiable smile turned to a grimace. "I have some news to share with you, but it would be best to discuss it in your study."

Panic gripped Darcy's heart. The study meant privacy. Richard had news he wished to keep private? "Is it an emergency? Is everyone well?"

"Yes, yes. Everyone is quite well. This is a matter of—" Richard's gaze landed on Snell, who regarded them with avid interest from the doorway. No doubt she would be happy for any crumbs of gossip she might share with the women of the neighborhood. "A matter of private business," Richard concluded.

"Very well." Darcy gestured to the stairs that led to his study.

"I will bring the gentlemen some tea!" Snell announced as they started to climb the steps. Darcy merely nodded, preoccupied by suppositions about what could have brought Richard all the way to Brighton.

Darcy's rooms were comfortable and spacious, decorated in the latest style, which was a bit ornate for his taste. He gestured for his cousin to proceed him into the study, which he had hardly used since he had been in residence.

Richard settled himself into a chair with a groan. No doubt he had ridden quite far today. Darcy took a couch near the unused fireplace.

"Your visits always bring me pleasure," Darcy told his cousin. "But your countenance suggests this visit is prompted by something worrisome."

"It is." Richard said nothing more while Snell bustled about the room, setting up a tea service between the two men. Silence reigned until she closed the door behind her.

Removing his hat, Richard ran a hand through his hair. "You are not wrong, Darce." He cleared his throat. "I was actually sent here…by the Home Office."

Darcy blinked. Well, that was unexpected news. "Why?"

Richard poured himself some tea. "As you know I have been on assignment there for a few months. Just yesterday we learned we had a spy: one Archibald Harrison."

Darcy winced. Few people knew that Richard was posted to the Home Office department that gathered intelligence for the war.

Discovering a spy spying on the spies would be a disaster. "Did you catch the man?"

Richard's hands clenched around his teacup. "Almost. But he slipped out of London before we could capture him. He had access to highly secretive information and therefore cannot be allowed to escape to France with it."

"Ah. You believe he is in Brighton."

His cousin nodded. "Smugglers leave Brighton for Calais with alarming regularity, and more than one agent has used that route to escape to France. Even worse, we know of at least one spy who sends information back to the emperor via such boats—and there may be an entire ring of spies."

Darcy whistled. "A ring!" He took a sip of tea while he considered this information. "So your superiors want you to capture the agent before he crosses the Channel?"

Richard hesitated and then spoke heavily as if the words were dragged from him. "Actually, there is a complication. I was hand-picked for this particular mission for a reason. We know the name of one spy in the ring. It is Wickham."

Darcy froze with a biscuit halfway to his mouth. His first impulse was to deny the allegation as absurd. While Wickham might be a scoundrel, surely he would not go so far as to betray his country. But the Home Office would not make such an accusation without hard evidence. Then he recalled the man's suspicious reaction to Denny's death. *Perhaps Wickham is capable of nearly anything.*

And Elizabeth's life is entangled with the wastrel's. Damnation! "How strong is the evidence against him?" Darcy asked, careful not to betray too much emotion.

"There is no doubt."

Darcy fought to control his temper. Wickham knew he was committing treason, and yet he dared to court Elizabeth! If only Darcy could race out of the door and strangle the man in his barracks… It would improve everyone's life.

But he would not do such a thing. Darcy was a civilized man who did not resort to violence, as much as he fantasized about the possibilities. He was a model of restraint. *Why is Richard staring at my hand?* Glancing down, Darcy found crumbs leaking out between his fingers onto the carpet. He had crushed the chocolate biscuit in his hand, squeezed it into tiny pieces. *Well, I suppose it is preferable to Wickham's skull.* Darcy carefully brushed the remaining crumbs onto the tea tray before speaking. "Damn Wickham! He causes no end of trouble."

Richard raised an eyebrow. "I expected you to be pleased. We have often fantasized about Wickham in prison. Now we have the means to achieve it."

Darcy cradled his head in his hands. "Under other circumstances I would be quite happy, but…" He made the hasty decision to take his cousin into his confidence. Richard would understand. "Miss Elizabeth Bennet is here in Brighton and has been keeping company with Wickham."

The other man grimaced. "I would have expected her to have superior discernment."

As would I.

"I would hate to see her fall prey to the scoundrel. Perhaps you should warn her."

"I have," Darcy said grimly. "She knows the entire story about Wickham…even Georgiana's role." This news prompted Richard's mouth to drop open. "She does not appear to value my advice, but she might listen to a warning from you."

Richard's brows drew together. "Why would she dismiss you? Surely your superior acquaintance with her family—"

Standing abruptly, Darcy paced to the window and stared out at the street. He must tell Richard the story, but he need not witness his cousin's reaction. "It is possible she believes I make such accusations out of jealousy." He bit out the words, hating that he must say them.

There followed such a long silence that Darcy wondered if he should confirm whether his cousin was still in the room. Finally, Richard spoke in a carefully neutral tone. "Does she have reason to believe you are jealous of Wickham?"

Darcy glowered at the house across the street. "I made her a proposal of marriage when we were visiting Rosings."

The gasp of surprise was quite audible. "And she refused you?"

Darcy simply nodded. "In part because of lies that Wickham told her about me."

"Damnation, Darcy! That is—!" Richard's voice broke off into an inarticulate grunt.

Darcy rushed on, wanting to divulge the whole sad story at once. "I subsequently wrote Elizabeth a letter describing my dealings with Wickham, including everything about Georgiana. She claims to have read it. But how can she tolerate breathing the same air as that wastrel, let alone allowing him to—?" He broke off; there was no reason to tell his cousin what he had seen in the colonel's garden.

Darcy finally peered back over his shoulder, anxious that the other man's face would be suffused with pity. But his cousin was staring at the carpet, deep worry lines etched on his face. "If we were discussing any other woman," Richard said slowly, "I might believe she simply demonstrates a lack of discernment, but not Miss Elizabeth—"

"Precisely!" Darcy exploded, starting to pace again. "It makes no sense."

Richard was silent as Darcy wore a path in the carpet. "I am concerned that perhaps Wickham has some hold over her family," Darcy said, not mentioning how a barmaid had suggested the idea. "Elizabeth denied it, but possibly there is something else that..."

"Hmm." Richard settled back in his chair. "If you told her of Wickham's treachery, would it alter her opinion?"

"I hope so." Darcy sighed and ran both hands through his hair. "But I do not know how I could convey the information. If only I could talk with her privately!"

Richard leaned forward in his chair. "You must speak with her—and soon—before she is caught up in his schemes."

"That had occurred to me," Darcy ground out through gritted teeth. "And there is an additional danger..." Hastily he informed his cousin of Denny's demise.

"Blast!" Richard slammed his fist onto the arm of the chair.

"It could be unrelated to Wickham's treachery," Darcy said.

"That is not likely."

"No."

Richard sighed. "The danger to Miss Bennet is greater than I originally realized."

"I would readily send her back to Hertfordshire in my own carriage," Darcy said. "But she must agree to such a journey—which she would only do with a good reason. And that requires an explanation given in a private conversation." Damn the rules of propriety! They even made it difficult to save a woman's life. "It will not be easy to find her alone."

Richard quirked a grin at his cousin. "Perhaps you could arrange a private conversation tonight."

Darcy shook his head. "I will have no opportunity to dine with the colonel."

"I was thinking about later in the night."

Darcy regarded him blankly.

"Come, Darce, surely you have— Don't tell me you have never climbed into a lady's bedchamber?"

"I have not," Darcy said stiffly. Many men of his acquaintance believed such activities to be good sport, relishing the danger, but Darcy had never counted himself among their number.

His cousin smirked. "Well, I have—more than once. I can give you some advice."

Was Richard serious? "Pray tell, did you ever climb into a lady's bedchamber when she did not anticipate your arrival and had expressed a distaste for your company?"

"Ah, no. I take your point." Richard frowned. "Those *are* different circumstances." They were both silent until his cousin spoke again. "Still, we dare not delay; tomorrow could be too late. A bedchamber *is* an excellent place for a private conversation."

Darcy was mildly scandalized. "Richard!"

"I will accompany you to the house and keep watch from below," Richard promised.

The very thought of discovery made Darcy shudder. "How reassuring."

"I *have* been professionally trained in detecting enemy combatants." When Darcy did not respond, Richard said, "I will happily listen to other ideas."

No doubt there were fifty far superior plans, but none came to mind. Finally, Darcy sighed. "If I do not have a better idea by this evening, we will try your plan. Heaven help me."

***

Darcy surveyed the back of Colonel Forster's house. It was a simple two-story brick structure with windows overlooking the garden. With the aid of a bright moon, he and Richard had observed the house for an hour and had seen no flickers of candlelight or signs of movement. They could reasonably assume everyone in the house was asleep.

Somewhere to their left a dog barked. Both Darcy and his cousin froze, but no one seemed to be inclined to investigate the cause.

"She mentioned that her window overlooks the garden," Darcy said in a low voice.

Richard peered at the two windows on the upper floor. "But which one is hers?"

Darcy took a deep breath. "I will simply have to guess." His cousin's eyes widened in alarm. "This was your idea," he reminded Richard.

"I am realizing how much simpler such a scheme is when the lady in question is eagerly awaiting your arrival." He fiddled with a button on his cuff, seeming uncertain about their plan for the first time since they had devised it.

Darcy did not respond. Despite his initial reluctance, he had concluded this was the best and fastest way to alert Elizabeth to the danger. Indeed, it might be the only way to ensure a private conversation; however, it was far from being the least risky plan available. Hopefully he could quickly convince Elizabeth not to scream. Or the night might end with him being arrested for trespassing—or perhaps being shot by Colonel Forster.

"I cannot decide who is a bigger fool: you for concocting this plan or me for acquiescing to it," he muttered to Richard.

"You are not foolish, just desperate to save Elizabeth's life."

"Desperate men are often fools," Darcy said, but Richard's reminder stiffened his resolve. This risk was necessary for the sake of Elizabeth's safety.

"I shall hoot like an owl if anyone approaches," Richard said in a low voice.

Darcy clapped his cousin on the shoulder. "If you ever need assistance eloping to Gretna Green, I will provide you with the same service."

Richard snorted. "This is a lot of trouble for someone who is not even eloping. While you are up there, ask if she would like to accompany you on a journey to Scotland. Kill two birds with one stone."

Darcy chuckled softly.

Then he returned his attention to the dark and silent house. The longer he waited, the more reasons he would find to abandon the venture. "I will go now." Creeping closer to the house, he examined the wall for convenient hand- and footholds, thankful that the garden fence would shield him from the street.

Hmm. If he climbed onto the portico over the back door, he could reach either upper-floor window and peer into the rooms. The sashes above the ground-floor windows would provide meager but adequate footholds to then climb into one of those rooms. As boys, he and Richard had delighted in climbing the outside of Pemberley, entering random rooms through unsecured windows. His mother had chastised them for startling the maids, but his father had been quietly amused.

Richard cupped his hands to give Darcy a boost up to the roof of the portico. Standing there and peering up at the windows, Darcy felt absurdly like the lover in some tawdry novel. Except that he had no romantic intentions—well, that was not the purpose of this visit. He only wanted to talk with Elizabeth, which somehow took the endeavor to new levels of absurdity.

Standing on the portico, Darcy peeked through one window, hoping to identify something through the glass. Fortunately, the curtains had not been drawn, revealing a bed draped in white. There appeared to be only one slumbering form, so the room did not belong to the colonel and his wife. But it could be Lydia's. If Darcy entered *her* room, he could be accused of compromising her and might be forced to make an offer of marriage. That thought was nearly enough to make him swear off the entire enterprise.

He examined the room for several minutes, but he could conceive of no way to ascertain the identity of the room's occupant without actually entering it. He would simply have to take his chances.

After saying a silent prayer, Darcy transferred his feet to the barely adequate foothold provided by the sash over the ground-floor window before carefully pushing open the upper window. Fortunately, it was not latched, and the pane swung inward noiselessly. It would be a tight squeeze, but there was sufficient space for him to enter the room. Darcy's feet pushed off the lower-level window sash as he simultaneously heaved himself up into the open window. Seconds later he was through the window, crouching on the worn carpet covering the floor and praying that nobody had heard his entrance.

Chapter Ten

The creaking of a floorboard roused Elizabeth to wakefulness. In the fog of sleep, she initially supposed the noise to be made by the colonel's maid, but why would the girl be by the window?

Opening her eyelids a crack, Elizabeth could see that the window was open and a dark figure was standing in front of it, silhouetted against the gray night sky. Her heart pounded against her ribs, and sweat dampened her palms. A man was in her room!

Closing her eyes again, she feigned sleep. Elizabeth was the only one who could stop him and alert the household to this threat. Frantically she recalled the objects on the table beside her bed. Could any be of use as a weapon?

Another creak of the floorboard announced the man's location: a few feet from the bed. The time to act was now. Simultaneously opening her eyes and thrusting out her arm, she grabbed the heavy brass candle holder from the table and hurled it at the dark figure.

The candle holder found its mark, striking him above the eye. He grunted and flinched away but did not fall. Elizabeth opened her mouth, preparing to cry out.

"Elizabeth, I pray you, do not scream!" the figure said in a familiar—albeit hushed—voice.

Shocked, she froze in the bed, taking a moment to recognize the voice. "Mr. Darcy?" Hurriedly she pulled the covers up to hide her chest; her modest nightrail was completely inadequate to shield her from his gaze.

What was happening? Surely this was a dream! Of all the men of her acquaintance, Mr. Darcy was the least likely to appear unexpectedly in a woman's bedchamber. But by the same token, he was unlikely to be here for some nefarious reason. Had the figure revealed itself to be Mr. Wickham, her screams would have awoken the entire town of Brighton.

"Eliz—Miss Bennet. Do not be alarmed," he urged in a low voice. "I wish you no harm."

She licked dry lips. "What *do* you wish with me?" After all, his idea of harm and hers could be quite different. If he were discovered in her bedchamber, it could do great damage to her reputation. Were he a different man, she might believe him to be executing an underhanded scheme to force her to marry him, but surely Mr. Darcy would not resort to such machinations.

"I merely wished to converse with you—in private."

She could not stifle a chuckle. "Surely there are less drastic ways to obtain a private audience."

"The subject is rather urgent."

"Urgent?" she echoed acidly. "Then by all means, welcome to my bedchamber."

Ignoring her sarcasm, he edged closer to the bed so he could lower his voice. "I believe Wickham presents a danger to you."

Elizabeth huffed out a breath. This again? He had risked her reputation to repeat a warning he had given that afternoon? She stifled an impulse to demand that he leave her room at once; no, the fastest way to be rid of him would be to let him speak his piece, refuse his entreaties to abandon Mr. Wickham, and *then* demand his departure.

"I see," she said slowly as she leaned toward the bedside table and lit the candle in the holder she had not thrown. The yellow glow revealed a small cut over one of Mr. Darcy's eyebrows. Elizabeth refused to feel regret; if he chose to break into her bedchamber, he must accept the consequences, including projectile candlesticks.

Still, it was most disconcerting having him loom over her while she crouched under the sheets. She slid to the far edge of the bed and gestured to the other side of the generously sized mattress. "This discussion may take a while. Why do you not seat yourself?"

Mr. Darcy regarded the space she indicated as he might a pit of venomous snakes. Elizabeth supposed it was rather a bold offer. But he had climbed through her window; surely he had forfeited any right to be shocked.

"Very well." He perched himself so gingerly on the far edge of the bed that he was in danger of slipping off at any moment. She no longer entertained any doubts about whether he had inappropriate intentions. In fact, another woman might have been insulted at his eagerness to avoid her proximity.

Once situated, however, Mr. Darcy appeared to be distracted. He stared at her face…no, her hair. It was unbound, a mass of dark curls spilling around her face and shoulders. He would only have seen her with her hair pinned into place; of course, he was staring. No doubt it was a mess of snarls. Her cheeks warmed with embarrassment; this was another reason gentlemen should not enter ladies' bedchambers unannounced.

No, he was the one who should be ashamed here, not Elizabeth. Lifting her chin, she tried to present herself with the composure of a lady while also shielding the front of her nightrail with the coverlet. "You came to issue a warning?" she prompted.

He started, colored, and quickly averted his eyes. "Yes, er"—he cleared his throat—"Wickham is dangerous. I am concerned about your continued association with him."

She sighed. "Mr. Darcy, I believe we have had this conversation previously."

His eyes returned to her, the flicker of the candlelight was reflected in their dark blue depths. "It has acquired new urgency with some news I received today. But first, you must tell me why you keep company with Wickham."

"You are not my commanding officer. I *must* do no such thing."

He flushed but did not desist. "Did he…force himself on you?"

"No!" Good Lord, had he actually envisioned such a horrible fate? How much anxiety had she occasioned the man?

His brows knitted together. "Then why do you seek his company?" His weight shifted, bringing him a little closer to her half of the bed. "You are too sensible, too clever to befriend a man you cannot respect."

Despite the uncomfortable situation, the compliments warmed her heart. Still, she did not reply; she could not give him the truth and did not want to dishonor him with a lie.

"Elizabeth?" he prompted. "You cannot tell me you are in love with him."

Her lips twisted in a rueful smile. "I suppose I cannot."

After another long pause he took a gentler tone. "You may confide in me. I will keep your confidences."

After a moment's consideration, she shook her head; they were not her confidences to share. While she did not believe Mr. Darcy had colluded with Mr. Wickham—otherwise he would hardly be in her bedchamber demanding answers—she knew the colonel would be particularly appalled if she shared the truth with this man.

Mr. Darcy swore under his breath, his hands clenching into fists. "Elizabeth, you do not understand the danger! You must avoid the man!"

"And I repeat that I do not take orders from you."

The man made a noise of frustration. "You do not know how dangerous he is!"

Elizabeth raised an eyebrow. Was it possible he spoke of more than Mr. Wickham's dissolute character? "You must be more specific, sir, if you wish to persuade me."

Mr. Darcy sighed, and his eyes roamed about the room as if the answers might hang on the walls. "Very well. The Home Office believes him to be an agent of Napoleon's."

"How do *you* know that?" The words burst from Elizabeth, immediately dashing any hope of concealing her shock.

Mr. Darcy's eyebrows shot up to his hairline. "You knew!"

There was no reason to dissemble now. Although she had betrayed her promise, she could not help experiencing a profound sense of relief. Lying to Mr. Darcy had been profoundly uncomfortable. Elizabeth nodded wearily. "Yes, Colonel Forster informed me in Meryton."

Understanding dawned on the man's face. "The colonel asked you to observe Wickham and report on his activities."

"Indeed. He hoped I could collect information about the man's operation."

Mr. Darcy blew out a long breath. "So you harbor no tender feelings for Wickham?"

"No, I assure you that pretending friendship has been a chore indeed."

"Why did you not inform me? I would have gladly rendered assistance!"

Her hands plucked at the coverlet. "I promised the colonel I would reveal the truth to no one."

"But—!"

His attitude irked Elizabeth. "You are not entitled to such information, as you are neither my father nor an agent of the Home Office."

Mr. Darcy's shoulders sagged. "You are correct…as usual, Miss Elizabeth. I wish to be concerned with your affairs, but I do not have that privilege."

Elizabeth immediately regretted the harshness of her words. "I do appreciate your concern for my wellbeing."

Leaning toward her, he clasped one of her hands in both of his. When had he come so near her on the bed? "'Concerned' does not adequately describe my disposition. I have been frantic with anxiety."

She could not help being touched by his devotion. "I did declare that I have no intention of eloping to Gretna Green with the scoundrel."

His warm hands squeezed her fingers. "If only that were my sole concern! But, Elizabeth, a man has been killed—perhaps by Wickham himself. And today Colonel Fitzwilliam arrived; the Home Office believes a French spy by the name of Archibald Harrison will contact Wickham about passage across the Channel. This is a very dangerous situation."

Elizabeth sobered. Here was grave news indeed, but it only reinforced the importance of her efforts. "I assure you that I will assume no untoward risks, and I am under Colonel Forster's protection."

Mr. Darcy scoffed. "He cannot watch over you every hour of the day."

"I assure you that I am exerting every possible caution."

"It is not sufficient! I have a carriage in Brighton. I beg you, allow me to send you home to Longbourn."

She withdrew her hand from his grasp. "No."

"I could not bear to lose you." His voice was rough with emotion.

The anguish in his voice gave her pause, but Elizabeth reminded herself that many in the war took far greater risks than she did. "No doubt many a soldier's wife has expressed such sentiments."

He frowned. "How is that relevant?"

Elizabeth pushed strands of hair from her eyes and continued in a softer voice. "I-I cannot fight as a soldier; this is the only way I may oppose the threat Napoleon represents to my country."

"B-But women do not fight in wars!" Her eyes must have been blazing, for Mr. Darcy immediately averted his gaze. After a long pause, he swallowed. "But I can see that such an argument will not dissuade you."

"Wise man." Her words were clipped with anger.

He said nothing for a full minute. "You believe in your purpose very strongly."

"I do."

Finally, his posture collapsed. "I am not pleased that you are stationed at the front lines, but I suppose that is not my decision to make."

"No." She softened her tone. "You are not responsible for me. If I am hurt, the fault is not yours."

He shook his head with a ghost of a smile on his lips. "I do not feel *responsible*."

"No?" Elizabeth took a minute to consider. His repeated intrusions had provoked such irritation that she had not devoted much thought to his motivations.

"No." He gave a mirthless laugh. "My feelings toward you are unchanged. I still love and admire you. Were something to happen to you, I would be...quite...bereft."

Elizabeth could not breathe. Somewhere in the back of her mind she must have guessed he was still in love with her, but her devotion to her mission made it easy to ignore. Or perhaps she had deliberately avoided any thoughts on the subject.

Her countenance must have registered her shock. Mr. Darcy edged closer to her on the bed. "I cannot tell you how relieved I am to learn you are not enthralled with Wickham." His voice was low and soft.

She gave him a shaky smile. "You must have thought me the worst sort of simpleton to befriend the man after reading your letter."

He closed his eyes briefly. "Worse. I thought I had lost any chance with you."

Again, the breath caught in her throat. "You wanted another chance with me?"

He chuckled softly. "I traveled to Longbourn for the purpose of offering an apology and requesting a chance to court you properly."

And instead he had learned I was intimately connected with Mr. Wickham. Oh. Her heart ached to think of the pain she had caused him.

"Is it too late for another chance?" Somehow he was now so close that his face was mere inches from hers.

This Darcy was very different from the stiff and arrogant man who had proposed so awkwardly at Hunsford. His voice was soft, and his head was low. Yes, he still experienced an impulse to issue orders, but he had attended to her chastisements and taken them to heart.

She had stuffed all her thoughts and feelings about Mr. Darcy into a box at the back of her mind. What would happen if she opened that box and allowed herself to explore the ripples of attraction she felt for him? Would those ripples become a wave? Would the wave drown her?

It was a profoundly reckless idea. Under the present circumstances, losing focus on her mission could lead to injury or death, and yet she could not banish Mr. Darcy from her thoughts. What would it be like to be courted by him? To truly discover his character? Over the past few days she had found hidden depths in the man, and she wanted to know more.

"No, it is not too late," she murmured.

Mr. Darcy's smile shone like the sun emerging from behind the clouds. "Elizabeth." He inhaled the syllables of her name as if they provided life-giving breath. He was moving toward her, and she was moving toward him. Their lips met somewhere in the space between—a joyous joining.

There was no comparison between this kiss and Mr. Wickham's. It would be like comparing a pile of rocks to Westminster Abbey. *Yes, this is how a kiss should be. This is the life-altering experience described in novels.* In no time at all, the kiss had stolen away her reason, her breath, her thoughts. Nothing remained but the sensation of his lips pressed to hers and the warmth of his body clinging to hers.

"Elizabeth…" he moaned against her mouth while his hands caressed her hair. "Just as soft as I had dreamed."

Another person had never stroked her hair before, and the experience was somehow both relaxing and stimulating, causing her to melt against him while also exciting her to deepen the kiss. Her fingers initiated their own exploration, plunging into his dark curls and stroking the strong curve of his jaw.

"I had lost hope of ever experiencing this," he murmured when they broke apart.

"You imagined it?" she asked—both surprised and flattered. How often had he thought about her?

"More times than I would care to confess." His fingers drifted lightly along the side of her neck, sending shivers down her back. She would have happily remained in this blissful place forever.

However, a sound intruded on her reverie. "Is that an owl hooting? I did not know any owls inhabited Brighton."

Mr. Darcy whirled around and leapt off the bed in one movement. Racing to the window, he unlatched it and threw it open. After a moment, she heard scraping sounds, male grunts and curses, and then thumps as someone climbed over the low sill of her window. Mr. Darcy assisted the unidentified man in entering her room. *If I had known I would entertain so many guests in the middle of the night, I would have prepared tea.*

Mr. Darcy quickly shut the window and drew the curtains closed. When the newcomer moved toward Elizabeth, she saw his face clearly for the first time. "Colonel Fitzwilliam!"

"Miss Bennet." The colonel executed a precise bow that struck her as rather excessive under the circumstances. "I apologize for my precipitous arrival. A night watchman was approaching the alley behind the garden, and I did not want my presence to be questioned. I gave my wayward cousin the signal"—he shot Mr. Darcy a sidelong glance—"but he dawdled a bit in opening the window."

Mr. Darcy's face was quite red. "I am sorry, Richard. I was distracted."

The colonel's eyes darted from him to Elizabeth. "I just bet." She colored as she imagined how disheveled they must appear.

Mr. Darcy huffed. "We have been discussing the danger that Wickham presents."

"And what did you conclude?"

No doubt the colonel believed Elizabeth should retreat to a safe location as well. Would Mr. Darcy admit Elizabeth had won that argument? He rubbed the back of his neck as he spoke. "Well, er, Eliz— Miss Elizabeth will remain in Brighton for now. She was recruited by Colonel Forster to report on Wickham's activities."

The colonel viewed her appraisingly. "So you are spying upon the spy? How clever of Forster; nobody suspects a woman of spying. More the fool they."

"But it is dangerous," Mr. Darcy interjected. "We do not know who killed Denny."

"Yes, dangerous," the colonel mused. Elizabeth braced herself for another argument about returning to Longbourn. Unexpectedly, he turned to his cousin. "We should devise a plan for ensuring her safety until her mission is completed."

Mr. Darcy appeared resigned rather than argumentative. "I will remain with Elizabeth, particularly when Wickham is in the vicinity, and serve as a kind of bodyguard." He turned anxious eyes to her. "If that is acceptable to you?"

Although pleased that he inquired, Elizabeth was prepared to object. Then she reconsidered; a protector might prevent Colonel Forster from returning her to Longbourn, and she was discovering she did not mind spending more time with Mr. Darcy.

"Very well." A broad smile was her reward. "I also believe you should meet with Colonel Forster in the morning and share your information. We can join forces."

"Such was my plan," Mr. Darcy said.

"Good."

The colonel peeked through the curtains. "The night watchman has departed, Darcy, and I suggest we make haste to leave as well. Every passing minute increases the odds of being detected." After his cousin's nod, the colonel opened the window and disappeared within seconds.

Mr. Darcy's gaze fixed on Elizabeth's lips; he obviously wanted to kiss her again but not when his cousin might see. Instead he took her hand and kissed the back. "I will see you tomorrow." His voice alone, low and husky, sent shivers along her spine.

A few seconds later he had departed, and Elizabeth was alone once more in her bedchamber.

***

Richard and Darcy were silent for several minutes as they hurried back to Darcy's lodgings. Darcy caught his cousin giving him sidelong stares more than once. Finally, he growled, "Say what you plan to say!"

Richard gave him a lopsided smile. "I sent you up there to *speak* with the lady, Darce, about a threat to her life. You were not supposed to make love to her."

"I did not make love—" Darcy sputtered.

Richard waggled a finger at him. "I saw the state of her hair. And your lips are still red and swollen." *They were?* He could not help touching a finger to his lips.

Darcy was not accustomed to defending himself from this kind of accusation. "It was the sheer relief, Richard. She does not love Wickham—and is working against him. The relief…lowered my inhibitions."

His cousin shook his head. "If you had been discovered dallying with her—"

"I am not dallying with her! I proposed marriage."

"Did she not refuse you?"

"I am attempting to change her mind."

"With kisses?"

Darcy bit back an angry retort. His cousin was right; his behavior had been inappropriate. *Perhaps there is sense behind the rule against visiting women in their bedchambers.* Fortunately, Elizabeth had not acted at all offended by the liberties he had taken. "You do not understand, Richard. She had— Her nightrail was— And then she—"

Richard snorted. "If a lady can render you this inarticulate, perhaps you are in love."

Darcy glowered at his cousin. "Really, it was her hair…I had never seen it unbound before…"

"Her hair is very beautiful." When Darcy scowled, Richard hastily added, "Not that I noticed…at all." After Darcy subsided, his cousin grinned. "I have never seen you so before. You are rather helplessly in love."

"Violently."

"Oh dear."

"Why do you sound so dismayed?"

His cousin sighed. "She has refused you once already."

A seed of doubt grew in Darcy's heart. "She allowed me to kiss her!"

"A handsome man appeared in her room at night, and she was swept away by passion. A kiss is not a promise of marriage." Darcy could not forget that his cousin had far more experience with midnight assignations than he did.

The warmth he had enjoyed since leaving the colonel's house was beginning to dissipate. Would Elizabeth kiss a man she did not intend to marry? Perhaps, if that man woke her unexpectedly in the middle of the night and demonstrated sincere concern for her wellbeing. She might be overwhelmed and confused and allow him liberties that she then regretted. When Darcy saw her in the morning, would she regard him with regret and shame? The thought cooled his ardor quickly.

"Did you learn anything else?"

"Hmm?"

"Did Miss Elizabeth relate anything else about Wickham beyond what we discussed in her bedchamber?"

Darcy tried to focus on the far more important subject of treason and threats to the nation. "I do not believe so."

Richard rubbed his chin. "I had no idea Wickham's commanding officer suspected him. I wonder if anyone in the Home Office knows? Damnation, this is a mess! The right hand doesn't know what the left is doing."

"We will sort it out with Forster in the morning."

They walked in silence for a minute. Darcy's thoughts constantly circled back to Elizabeth. "I wish I had convinced her to return to Hertfordshire, but she is determined to do what she can for country and crown."

"Admirable."

"Foolhardy," Darcy growled. "She risks her life."

Richard considered for a moment. "If the woman were easily cowed, she would not hold your interest. You have had years to fall in love, but the first woman to win your heart is the one who exhibits bravery and cleverness beyond the normal bounds. I do not believe this to be a coincidence."

They had arrived at his lodgings. Darcy paused with his hand on the doorknob. "What are you proposing I do?"

Richard clapped him on the shoulder. "I am suggesting, my friend, that you accept the bad as you embrace the good."

They spoke no more, but for the remainder of the night, Darcy considered his cousin's words.

Chapter Eleven

Mr. Wickham was his usual gallant self the following morning—
and it turned Elizabeth's stomach. Greeting her with a smirk in Colonel
Forster's drawing room, he kissed her hand and gave extravagant praise of
her beauty. Sitting beside her, he murmured asides under the noise of the
general conversation—provided by Colonel and Mrs. Forster, Lydia, and
two of Mr. Wickham's fellow officers.

The room was rather crowded.

Elizabeth had lain awake for a long time after Mr. Darcy's
departure and then slept fitfully; the resulting fatigue caused her to be
restless and irritable. Pretending passion for Mr. Wickham was growing
increasingly difficult. She hoped the nausea was not evident on her face.

Memories of the previous night rendered the deception more
difficult. In the early hours of the morning, she had kissed Mr. Darcy on
her bed, and now she was flirting with Mr. Wickham. Any action would
be wrong. If she smiled invitingly at Mr. Wickham, she betrayed the
feelings beginning to develop between her and Mr. Darcy. But if she
beheld the officer with indifference, then she might lose an opportunity to
collect valuable information.

Mr. Darcy understands my mission; he shares my goals.

The reminder helped alleviate some guilt, but the sense of betrayal
lingered. It had been an enormous relief to tell the man the truth, but it
created new complications.

Mr. Darcy and his cousin had not yet arrived to speak with the
colonel, and Elizabeth anticipated their entrance with no small anxiety.
Would Mr. Wickham be suspicious of Colonel Fitzwilliam's sudden
appearance? Might he reveal a clue about the location of the French spy?

Elizabeth was eager to be finished with this deception. Once they
caught the agent, Colonel Forster could arrest Mr. Wickham and Elizabeth
could return home.

In the meantime, she was virtually imprisoned in this drawing
room, where the colonel was telling a longwinded story from his early
days in the militia about a donkey and a goat. Everyone listened with
polite attention—no doubt hoping, like Elizabeth, that the tale would
prove to be moderately entertaining at some point.

While everyone's attention was engaged, Elizabeth took the
opportunity to scrutinize Mrs. Forster. Since the day at the beach, she had

not noticed any signs of the lady's particular regard for Mr. Wickham; perhaps their conversation had been nothing more than the usual insipid banter the colonel's wife habitually exchanged with the officers. They did not steal furtive glances at each other or seek out private conversations.

Mrs. Forster flirted with every man within reach; there was no reason to believe she preferred Mr. Wickham or enjoyed an improper relationship with him. Now Elizabeth was pleased she had said nothing of the incident to the colonel. He had enough reasons for concern.

When would Mr. Darcy arrive?

The sound of the front door opening momentarily raised her hopes, only to have them dashed when Dawkins opened the door and addressed Mr. Wickham. "A boy brought this note for you. Said it was urgent."

Mr. Wickham took the note from the woman and retired to the far-less-crowded front hallway to read it. When he stepped back into the room, everyone watched him expectantly.

"What is it, Wickham?" the colonel asked amiably. "It had better not be a love letter!"

The other officers chortled, glancing at Elizabeth, whose face heated. Uncharacteristically distracted, Mr. Wickham did not react to the jibe. "My friend, Henry Knox, has taken a fall, and his mother writes to beg my help. She cannot even lift him in and out of bed."

"Fall, eh?" One of the officers laughed. "Probably foxed, he was."

"Knox?" the colonel said. "He is not one of our company."

"No, he's a local man I knew as a boy. Might I go and help her, sir?"

"Very well." The colonel waved dismissively. "I have no need of you this morning. Go, be a good Samaritan to your friend." Additional jibes and laughter followed Mr. Wickham as he exited the drawing room.

While the conversation immediately turned to various types of muskets, Elizabeth considered the incident. She did not for one moment believe the note had been about an ailing friend. Mr. Wickham was not the sort of "friend" one sought out for assistance; he was too selfish. More likely he had been contacted by the traitor who wanted transport to France.

She tried to catch the colonel's eye to learn if he shared her concern, but the man was deeply involved in the conversation and paid her no heed. If she remained here, Elizabeth would miss the chance to discover the spy's location. It was too good an opportunity to lose.

She stood quickly and slipped from the room. Few people noticed, and the conversation continued unabated. The front hallway was empty as she rushed out of the door and onto the street.

Fortunately, Mr. Wickham had not traveled far. Lifting her skirts, Elizabeth hurried after him, catching his elbow to get his attention. "Mr. Wickham, I had a thought! Perhaps I can come with you and help you nurse your poor friend. I am certain he would improve with a woman's touch."

The officer hastily concealed his initial impatience with a smile. "That is a very generous offer, but I don't believe it would be appropriate to have a young lady accompany me there."

Conjuring an image of Lydia at her most flirtatious, Elizabeth pasted on a coy smile. "But I will not be any trouble at all. I will help!"

Although Mr. Wickham seemed a bit dazzled, he shook his head. "You are generosity itself, but the colonel would not be pleased if I spirited you away without his permission—and Knox does not live in a neighborhood that is appropriate for young ladies to visit."

Elizabeth pouted and gave a reluctant nod, allowing Mr. Wickham to march away from her with a determined stride. In truth, she had not expected that ploy to be successful. However, the officer's determination to refuse her company rather confirmed her suspicion about whom he was meeting.

She waited until he was several streets away and began to follow.

***

A series of unfortunate delays caused Darcy and Richard to arrive later at the colonel's house than they had planned. When the housekeeper opened the door, they found a distressed and hurried Colonel Forster donning his hat in the front hallway.

"Mr. Darcy." He gave a short nod. "I am afraid I have urgent business, but my wife is in the drawing room if you would like to—"

Darcy suppressed a flicker of irritation; he could not imagine that any business of the colonel's could be more pressing than theirs. "We must speak with you immediately," Darcy interrupted. "This is Colonel Fitzwilliam, currently on assignment with the *Home Office*." The last words had their desired effect; the colonel stilled and stared at Richard.

"Is there somewhere private we may talk?" Darcy's cousin asked.

"Of course." Colonel Forster led the way to his private study where he positioned himself behind the desk. Nobody sat.

Richard carefully closed the door before speaking. "I am in Brighton seeking a French agent who infiltrated the Home Office and escaped with sensitive information. We believe he is in Brighton and will try to contact Wickham for help in crossing the Channel."

Colonel Forster exhaled. "You are aware of Wickham's treachery."

"Yes, but I did not know you were also pursuing Wickham until Miss Bennet informed us yesterday." Darcy hoped the colonel would not inquire as to how or when they had spoken with Elizabeth.

The other man slammed his hand on the desk. "Damn the Home Office! They cannot coordinate even the simplest things."

Richard smiled with no warmth. "I don't disagree. However, at the moment my purpose is to locate Wickham. If I follow him, perhaps he will lead me to Harrison."

Colonel Forster ran fingers through his thinning hair. "There is a dilemma. Wickham was here on a morning visit with some other officers, but he received a letter—supposedly about a sick friend—and departed rather abruptly. At the time I barely noted it, but now I believe the odds are good that it pertains to Harrison."

"Blast!" Richard said. "If only we had arrived a little earlier."

The colonel shook his head rather frantically. "You don't understand. Miss Elizabeth was in the drawing room as well." A cold feeling started to grow in the pit of Darcy's stomach. "She slipped out of the room immediately after Wickham left and did not return. When you arrived, I was preparing to go in search of her."

"She went with him!" Darcy exclaimed.

"Or she is following him," the colonel said.

Darcy silently agreed that was the more likely explanation.

"Do you have any conjectures as to where Wickham might have gone?" Richard asked.

The colonel sighed. "No. If the note was from Harrison, they could be meeting anywhere in Brighton."

"And Elizabeth with them!" Any number of ghastly outcomes occurred to Darcy. Wickham had probably killed once; he would not hesitate to do so again. Darcy wanted to pace, but the room was too cramped, so he found himself shifting restlessly on his feet.

The colonel regarded him with narrowed eyes. "Pardon my curiosity, but what precisely is *your* interest in this matter, Mr. Darcy?"

They had no time to waste on idle curiosity! Darcy suppressed an impulse to shout at the man. As Elizabeth's guardian, the colonel had a right to know, and they would be working together. "Colonel Fitzwilliam is my cousin, and Wickham has been long known to my family—having caused us many difficulties."

Colonel Forster's skeptical expression suggested that Darcy had not sufficiently explained his reaction. "Also"—Darcy blew out a breath; he hated laying his affairs bare before strangers—"I am hoping to persuade Miss Elizabeth to become my wife."

"You are?" The colonel's eyebrows shot upward. "But I thought her family…"

"Yes?" Darcy watched the other man steadily, daring him to finish the sentence. Did he have the audacity to find Elizabeth unworthy? When the colonel did not continue, Darcy explained, "I traveled to Brighton for the sole purpose of protecting her from Wickham, since I knew him to be a blackguard of the first order."

Forster stiffened. "I assure you that I would not allow any harm to come to her."

Darcy bared his teeth, finished with any pretense of politeness. "With all due respect, sir, I am more familiar with Wickham's machinations than you are."

"I was tasked with her safety by her father," the colonel growled.

"Yes, you were. And where is she now?"

Forster abruptly deflated, collapsing into the chair behind his desk. "Very well. Point taken." He massaged his forehead with one hand. "What should our first step be?" he asked Richard. "Should we seek Harrison or Wickham first?"

Darcy slammed his fist on the desk's mahogany surface, causing Forster to flinch. "Our first task is finding Miss Bennet. She could be in grave danger!"

Forster blinked. "Yes, yes, of course. We can search the town for her." He stood, no doubt eager to quit Darcy's presence.

Darcy's shoulders relaxed fractionally. "Do you have men who may assist with the search?"

The man paused on his way to the door. "A few. But it's a delicate situation; I can only share this information with men I can trust."

Darcy nodded. "Then let us collect them so we may start searching."

***

Elizabeth was certain the man she observed was Harrison. The stranger had met with Mr. Wickham near one edge of the Steyne. After a quick and animated conversation, the two men had parted, leaving in opposite directions. Hoping to discover where Harrison was staying, she had elected to follow him.

He was a small, thin man with a narrow face and nervous eyes. Wearing a brown coat and equally brown hat, he melted indistinguishably into the crowds of visitors thronging the busy streets near the green. Following him had been difficult, but Elizabeth had managed to keep pace without alerting him to her presence

He came to an intersection of several streets, teeming with carriages, horses, and people walking in every direction. With only a cursory glance around, the man dove directly into the melee. *Very well.* Elizabeth took a deep breath and followed.

Only to find her way blocked by a man on horseback.

Huffing with impatience, she tried to duck around the rear of the horse, but the animal moved backward to block her again. Elizabeth shot an irritated glare up at the rider, only to find she was glaring at the face of Mr. Darcy.

"That is Harrison!" she hissed at him, pointing to the man. "He is escaping!"

Mr. Darcy shook his head. "Finding Mr. Harrison is not your responsibility. It is too dangerous."

She did not have time to argue. Growling at Darcy under her breath, she feinted left. As the horse moved to block her, she jumped to the right, skirting around the horse's rear and plunging into the intersection. But Harrison was gone. Elizabeth turned in a circle, peering down every street, but there was no sign of a short man in a brown coat. Blast!

Before she could decide on her next move, a hand grabbed her elbow, and Mr. Darcy pulled her out of the street to relative safety under a shop's awning; his horse was tied up nearby. She wrenched her arm from his grasp. "Do not lay hands on me, sir!"

He immediately backed away, conspicuously not touching her, but his stormy expression suggested an apology would not be forthcoming. "What were you about?" he demanded gruffly.

Elizabeth spoke through gritted teeth. "I hoped to learn where Mr. Harrison lodges so Colonel Fitzwilliam could apprehend him."

"Colonel Forster would not want you to do something so dangerous."

She put her hands on her hips. "It is a curious thing, but I do not recall putting myself under Colonel Forster's command—or yours, sir!" Blood was boiling in her veins, and it was all she could do to keep her voice low. "You are in no position to make decisions for me. You are not my father. You are not even my host!"

Mr. Darcy's mouth opened and then closed again.

If she remained, there was a grave danger Elizabeth might say something she would regret. "Good day." Whirling around, she strode away from him as rapidly as she could manage.

"Elizabeth, wait!" She did not slow her pace, but Mr. Darcy hurried to catch up with her. "How did you know that man was Harrison?"

"I do not. Not for certain," she admitted. "But Mr. Wickham met with the man when he was supposed to visit a sick friend. He must be connected to his nefarious activities somehow. They did not speak long, and I suspect they made plans to rendezvous tonight. But I could not hear what they said." She was still walking but had slowed her pace. Her anger at Mr. Darcy should not interfere with the larger mission.

The next minute passed in silence as they marched toward Colonel Forster's house. Then Mr. Darcy cleared his throat. "I apologize. I should have at least ascertained your purpose before stopping you. I have been seeking you for more than an hour, imagining the many different ways you might have been hurt. I reacted rather badly."

As Elizabeth paused on a street corner, she examined his face. Worry lines were etched around his mouth, and his eyes were shadowed by dark circles. "I accept your apology." His shoulders sagged. "However, I will not—I *cannot*—countenance a friend who does not trust my judgment—even in matters concerning my own safety."

His eyes searched hers for a moment. No doubt he understood—as she intended—that she would refuse to marry such a man. "I understand." He nodded slowly. "I will attempt to keep my…impulses under regulation."

It was a remarkable promise from a man like Mr. Darcy. The master of Pemberley was certainly accustomed to having his own way in all things. "I thank you, sir. Now, we should return to Colonel Forster's house to discuss what I have learned."

Chapter Twelve

As they strolled back to Forster's house, Elizabeth took Darcy's arm while he held the reins for the horse plodding behind them. Elizabeth was uncharacteristically silent. Was she still fuming about his interference, or was she more concerned about losing Harrison?

There was no question that he had made a mull of it.

He had been aware—in a rather theoretical way—that women did not like being told what to do. However, he had believed that the rule applied to situations like how to wear their hair. Or who to befriend. Or what to serve for dinner. Darcy had been concerned for Elizabeth's safety! Surely different rules should apply.

Apparently not.

He was not a stupid man. It had been drilled into him from a young age that he must protect women, but he could understand how Elizabeth might see his protective instincts as…meddlesome…high-handed…condescending.

I have much to atone for.

His first impulse had been to defend himself, but he had suppressed it. He was trying to demonstrate that he could attend to Elizabeth's rebukes and change his behavior. It was the only way to win her hand—and her heart.

Elizabeth believed her life was hers to do with as she pleased—much as most men did. It was only fair, and yet he struggled with the idea; it was not how he was accustomed to thinking of women. Yet he needed to be comfortable with the idea if he wanted her to marry him—to love him.

I should be grateful she accepted my apology. He was also slightly heartened that she had essentially warned him she would not marry a man who behaved in a high-handed way. Such a warning would be entirely unnecessary if she believed she would never entertain another proposal from him.

Perhaps I am no longer the last man in the world she would consider marrying. That thought alone put more spring in Darcy's step.

Darcy tied up his horse outside Forster's house, and they hurried through the front entrance. Both colonels had recently returned and convened in the study. They were relieved to see Elizabeth and eagerly listened to her report. When she described the man she had seen, Richard nodded vigorously. "Yes, that is Harrison."

"Very well, we know Harrison has made contact with Wickham." Forster sank into his chair and gestured for the others to take seats. "What should we do next?"

"I could exert some pressure on Wickham. With the right incentive—say, leniency in sentencing—he might reveal the plans," Richard said.

Forster grimaced. "That is only possible if we can find Wickham. The man has not returned to his barracks. I have someone watching out for him, but I would imagine he'll remain inconspicuous until this situation is resolved. Getting Harrison to France is a more important task than Wickham and his friends have ever undertaken before."

"Harrison will ship out tonight if he can," Richard observed.

"But from where?" Darcy asked.

"The cave!" Elizabeth exclaimed, exchanging a look with Colonel Forster.

He nodded. "Indeed." His eyes fell on Richard and Darcy. "Miss Elizabeth induced Wickham to show her the location of a cave in the cliffs to the east of Brighton. I surveyed the location myself, and there is no doubt it is being used by smugglers. It is far enough from the town that it would make an excellent point of departure for a small boat."

"Good work." Richard nodded approvingly at Elizabeth. "When would they depart?" he asked Forster.

The other man stroked his chin. "No doubt they will sail at night. The tide will be high at ten o'clock tonight. I could lead a team of men…recruit a few officers I may trust."

Richard was on the edge of his seat. "I will accompany you. I have longed to apprehend Wickham, and Harrison must be my prisoner. The Home Office wants me to bring him in for questioning."

Forster nodded. "I will be happy for any assistance."

"We must be in place by nine so as to arrive undetected," Richard said.

The two soldiers shook on the plan.

"Wickham has grown even more lax in his duties recently," the colonel said. "He may be planning to accompany Harrison to France. It is only a matter of time before he retreats across the Channel to enjoy whatever gold Napoleon has promised him."

"Does he guess the Home Office suspects him?" Elizabeth asked.

Forster shrugged. "Perhaps, or perhaps he is staying one step ahead of his creditors. I am sure he works with at least one other person. I had hoped to learn how he was obtaining such secretive information. Did he give you any clues, Miss Elizabeth?"

She shook her head. "He surprised me sometimes about what he knew about troop movements, but I never witnessed him visiting your study."

"Was he intercepting your post?" Darcy asked.

"Possibly. I will have someone investigate it." Forster turned to Elizabeth. "Miss Bennet, fortunately I believe your part in this scheme is at an end, but your assistance has been invaluable."

She smiled and blushed. "I am pleased I could be of help."

Richard frowned. "Miss Elizabeth, is it possible Harrison noticed you following him?"

Her forehead furrowed. "I tried to be discreet, but at times it was difficult to remain concealed. So I believe it is possible."

Darcy exchanged an anxious glance with his cousin, but before he could say anything, Forster spoke up. "Then I would like you to remain out of sight for the remainder of the day. If you encountered Wickham or Harrison, you could be in jeopardy."

Elizabeth grimaced, but she nodded. "I will."

The militia officer turned a slightly less benevolent expression on Darcy. "I thank you for the role you have played, but I do not believe we will be in need of your further assistance."

Darcy raised an eyebrow. "My primary aim has been to keep Miss Bennet safe. I am happy to leave the apprehension of spies to professional soldiers."

The colonel nodded; no doubt he was relieved not to have civilians bumbling about and complicating what had become a military operation. And with that, the war council was adjourned.

***

Elizabeth had worried that Mr. Darcy would insist on being her constant companion and guardian for the remainder of the day. However, he merely extracted a promise from her not to leave the colonel's house. Since he planned to be absent much of the day, the colonel had arranged for a few trusted officers to guard his house until the men were captured.

She chafed at the restrictions but reminded herself of the dangers; it appeared more and more probable that Mr. Wickham had killed Mr.

Denny. She shivered, recalling how she had been alone with the officer: a man who was capable of murdering such a friendly, affable man. Happily, everything would be resolved by tonight. The colonels would arrest the traitors, and Elizabeth would return to Hertfordshire.

And what would happen with Mr. Darcy? Elizabeth could not say. She was unsure what she would even like to occur.

An entire day spent indoors did wear on her nerves. She embroidered until the sight of a needle nauseated her and drank enough tea to float a ship. On a day when Elizabeth would have been happy for some company, Mrs. Forster was out of town visiting friends. Surprisingly, Lydia had not been invited, so the youngest Miss Bennet lolled about the drawing room complaining of boredom and eating biscuits until she retired to her bedchamber with a stomach ache.

The forced inactivity provided Elizabeth with far too much time to think. What was Mr. Darcy doing at that moment? Was he thinking of her? Would he accompany them home to Longbourn? Would he continue to court her?

How her sentiments had altered since Kent! Most of her thoughts about him were now quite positive. Yes, he had been high-handed, but he had also listened to her remonstrances and exhibited a willingness to change—a rare characteristic in a man, or indeed any person. He wanted to improve his behavior—for her sake. Forget flowers and jewels; Elizabeth would defy any woman to guard her heart in such circumstances.

Oh! I am beginning to fall in love with Mr. Darcy!

Her embroidery fell, forgotten, into her lap.

In love? With Mr. Darcy? Is it possible?

Gently she probed her sentiments as one might explore a sore tooth—and concluded that not only was it possible, it was likely.

Being in his presence so frequently had shown Elizabeth how much pleasure she derived from his company. He was witty and cultured. He had good morals and a strong character. He was, in fact, everything a gentleman should be. And now Elizabeth was no longer blind to how much he cared for her. He was concerned for her safety, her happiness, and her good opinion, demonstrating his love in many ways.

And she was beginning to reciprocate.

Her hand flew to her mouth. What could this mean? She had assumed that he wooed her with the intention of making another offer of marriage, but what if he did not? The very thought made her shiver.

On the other hand, she should be careful what she wished for. Did she truly want another proposal? It would only make sense if she planned to give him a different response from the previous proposal. Would she?

Elizabeth pictured Mr. Darcy making another offer, and she imagined herself opening her mouth to respond with…

Here, her imagination failed her. She did not know her response. *I suppose it is fortunate he has not asked the question.*

When he had first proposed, Elizabeth had believed he could not possibly have made a worse choice for his wife. Now she realized they were far better suited than she had initially understood. Perhaps he had been right about their compatibility in marriage as well.

Elizabeth passed much of the afternoon staring out of the window and accomplished very little of her embroidery. The two sisters shared a dinner of cold meat alone. Lydia's conversation primarily consisted of laments over Mrs. Forster's continued absence and their confinement within the house. Since Lydia remained unaware of the heightened sense of danger, the restrictions had chafed even more for her. Elizabeth contributed little to the conversation as she was caught up in musings about French spies and a certain man from Derbyshire.

Mr. Darcy called at half past eight; by then Elizabeth was prepared to fling herself into his arms if he would only take her from the house. After a long day of inactivity, even Lydia was happy to see someone "so horribly dull." At about nine o'clock, Mr. Darcy extended an offer to take Elizabeth for a walk through the town. By now Mr. Wickham and his cohorts would be on their way to the cliffside cave, so they would present no danger.

Elizabeth accepted eagerly and held her breath as Mr. Darcy politely extended the offer to Lydia, but she wrinkled her nose and declined. Apparently, she had a limited tolerance for Mr. Darcy's company. Elizabeth could not feign disappointment as she was happy to escape Lydia's complaints for a while.

The sun set late at this time of year, and it was still quite light when they departed from the house. Warm and humid, the air moved sluggishly, so Elizabeth suggested they make their way to the beach, which always enjoyed a good breeze.

They first strolled along St. James Street, a grand promenade that ran parallel to the beach. Only a single row of houses and shops separated the lane from the beach, and several cross streets led directly to the sand.

A popular site for after-dinner perambulations, the lane was a place to see the "right" sort of people—and to be seen in turn.

Mr. Darcy seemed content to allow Elizabeth to lead the way. She admired the silk displayed in one shop window and examined ribbons at another, but Mr. Darcy's company was far more interesting than the wares in any shop.

Soon weary of being jostled by the crowds, Elizabeth found herself yearning for a little more privacy to enjoy Mr. Darcy's company. "Might we walk on the beach?" she asked him. "If it is not too much trouble." She knew that many people did not enjoy such excursions, particularly when they got sand in their shoes.

"Of course." He smiled. "The beach is one of my favorite places." This made Elizabeth smile in return. "If we turn right at the next corner, we will arrive at the beach directly."

However, before they reached the next corner, they became aware of a commotion ahead of them on St. James Street. The crowds had ceased moving as people gawked at a small group moving slowly in their direction. As the group grew closer, Elizabeth discerned two men leading the way in elaborate livery, carrying both swords and pistols. She squinted, trying to make out the design of the livery, and then gasped.

"It seems the prince regent will be gracing us with his presence," Darcy murmured in her ear.

Elizabeth's stomach fluttered. The prince regent's presence in Brighton had been the subject of many dinner table conversations at the colonel's house, but all had agreed that they were unlikely to glimpse him except as a face in a passing carriage. Accounts about the prince were numerous and often contradicted each other; Elizabeth was eager to learn the truth for herself.

Now she could glimpse the figure of the prince behind the guards. Having seen engravings and reproductions of portraits of the prince, Elizabeth had thought he was not a particularly handsome man. Now she knew that the artists had been generous.

He was…well, no other word could describe his gait except waddling. She believed she had never seen such a…rotund personage. He wore a suit of light blue silk and an enormous number of jewels—both on his fingers and around his neck—that somehow magnified his size. His eyes protruded slightly, and his jowls flapped with every step. With a red face and perspiration dripping into the neck of his cravat, he seemed to veer precariously close to the edge of an apoplectic fit. Obviously, years of a self-indulgent lifestyle had taken a toll on the man's health.

He leaned on a jewel-encrusted walking stick in one hand while a well-dressed, bosomy lady held his other arm. She appeared to be propping him up rather than using his arm to steady herself. This must be Mrs. Fitzherbert; she had been the prince's mistress for many years.

Two liveried servants followed behind the prince, anxiously scrutinizing his every step. Perhaps their job was to catch him in case he should fall, although they hardly appeared equal to the task. Two additional guards made up the rear of the procession.

The prince regent appeared to be every inch the indolent and dissolute man described by rumors and broadsides—a man who had earned his subjects' disrespect and scorn. As he passed, many people bowed or curtsied—and many did not—but he took no notice either way.

As the procession grew closer, Elizabeth tried to recall what she had learned about court manners. The presence of royalty required a special kind of curtsey, but she did not remember the precise form—or indeed if anyone had taught it to her. She had never anticipated having a need for it.

However, all the prince's efforts were focused on walking in the heat; he was unlikely to notice if she curtsied incorrectly. With his head held high, his eyes touched the crowd only briefly, and he made no effort to interact with the bystanders.

In her mind, Elizabeth rehearsed the curtsey she believed to be the correct one and prepared to make it. But as the entourage neared them, the prince called a halt. "Darcy? Is that you? Darcy?"

Chapter Thirteen

Mr. Darcy took a deep breath, stepped forward, and made a low bow. Behind him, Elizabeth quickly made her curtsey. When Mr. Darcy straightened, he spoke in a solemn, even tone. "Your Highness, you look well." *Ah*, thought Elizabeth, *he does know how to lie.*

"Thank you, but Brighton is deuced hot this time of year!" the prince grumbled as a servant handed him a handkerchief to mop his brow. "I would have remained in the Pavilion, but Maria did so long for a walk." He absently patted the woman's hand where it rested on his arm.

"It is a nice evening for a walk," Mr. Darcy said.

"I did not know you were in Brighton." The prince's tone was almost peevish, as though Mr. Darcy was obligated to keep him informed of his whereabouts. "Where are you staying?"

"The Crescent, Your Highness."

"Not a bad place. You should come to dine at the Pavilion." The prince made a grand, expansive gesture. "I am contemplating more renovations to the place. As you know, Moghul and Indian designs are the very height of fashion. My architect—Nash is his name—has designed an addition with these wonderful turrets and domes. I could show you the plans!"

"That would be delightful." Mr. Darcy's voice was carefully neutral.

The prince wheezed a bit. "Yes, yes, yes, yes." He teetered on his elegantly shod feet; for a moment it appeared the servants might be pressed into service to catch him. However, with the help of his mistress and the cane, the prince regained his balance. "Perhaps I should sit for a while." He glanced about, but they were in the midst of a cobblestone street, now closed to carriage traffic; no benches or chairs were in evidence. "Hastings, find me a chair."

One of the servants hurried into the nearest house, emerging immediately with a rather plain wooden chair that he set behind the prince, who sank into it with a sigh. "Damned gout!" he exclaimed. "Sea bathing is supposed to be beneficial for it, but I do not know."

He peered up at Mrs. Fitzherbert, standing by his side. "Hastings, obtain a chair for Maria." The servant repeated the process, retrieving a chair from the same house and setting it beside the prince's. Standing in their doorway, the owners of the house were peering wide-eyed at the spectacle. They did not appear particularly well off, and Elizabeth wondered if their household owned additional chairs or if the prince had commandeered their entire supply. *I hope the prince would not think to order chairs for us!*

Now that he was seated, the prince seemed to be of a more amiable disposition, arranging his face in a rather grotesque smile. "Who were you walking with just now?" he asked Mr. Darcy. "Do you have a wife?"

"No, Your Highness." Mr. Darcy gestured for Elizabeth to come forward. "This is my friend, Miss Elizabeth Bennet." She made another awkward curtsey, devoutly hoping it was the proper one.

The prince's attention immediately drifted away; evidently Mr. Darcy's friends were not of interest. Seconds later, the prince was seized by a great coughing fit that shook his entire frame. Mrs. Fitzherbert and the servants bustled about, offering water—or some other liquid—from a flask and patting his back, but their efforts served no obviously beneficial purpose.

After many long minutes, the prince was finally able to speak again, with a wheezier and hoarser voice. "Damned consumption! It never seems to improve."

"I am very sorry to hear that," Mr. Darcy said.

"Yes…well…" The prince waved irritably, obviously finished with the conversation. "I would like some cake. Hastings, find somewhere that will give me some cake."

The servant evinced some surprise at this order but immediately ran down the street in search of cake. Elizabeth hoped the man would buy it from an establishment that sold cake rather than stealing it off the table of some hapless family.

The prince pointed to Darcy. "Contact my secretary about a dinner engagement, and I shall show you those designs. Such turrets! Such domes! It will be quite grand!"

"I will," Mr. Darcy said.

"Be sure to take your lady here to the beach. It is very pretty at this time of day," the prince wheezed.

"We were going there just this minute," Mr. Darcy said.

"I should love to walk along the beach!" Mrs. Fitzherbert sighed.

"Would you, Maria?" The prince gave her a fond smile. "You know how I hate the sand and stones, but perhaps after I have rested, we may take a short walk on the beach."

"That would be most delightful!" She beamed at him.

The prince waved at Mr. Darcy. "Perhaps we shall see you at the beach by and by."

Recognizing their dismissal, Mr. Darcy bowed again, took Elizabeth's arm, and set a brisk pace along the street, not slowing until they had turned the corner. Once they were out of the prince's sight, he gave a long exhale and allowed his shoulders to sag. He shot Elizabeth an anxious look. "I apologize for subjecting you to such an…awkward situation."

She shrugged. "Lydia will be quite jealous that I have met the prince regent and she has not."

"I suppose. I would happily send her in my stead to the Pavilion."

"How are you acquainted with the prince?"

Mr. Darcy removed a handkerchief from his pocket and wiped his brow. "I am not—not really. We have met upon a few occasions. My father lent cash to the king some fifteen or twenty years back; as a result, our family was often invited to state occasions. I was fairly young at the time and found them quite tedious."

"You would probably find them tedious today as well."

"Ha! Probably." He carefully folded the handkerchief and replaced it in his pocket. "The debts were repaid, my father died, and the king…grew ill. Intercourse between our families dwindled, and I did nothing to encourage it. I did encounter the prince at a ball some five years ago, and he was eager to talk about 'old times.' Still, I am surprised he recognized me."

Elizabeth was not quite so surprised. Mr. Darcy was a striking man. Even someone as self-centered as the prince regent would find him remarkable. "Do you believe he will actually invite you for dinner?"

Mr. Darcy sighed. "I suppose it is possible; he is obviously eager to share his architect's renovation plans. I must contact His Highness's secretary; that was practically a royal command. However, it is just as likely the prince will have lost interest in two days' time." His tone suggested that he would prefer to be forgotten. She understood; excessive royal scrutiny could be unnerving, particularly from such a prince.

He took her hand and set it firmly back on his arm. "But enough of princes and royalty. Let us walk along the beach and think on pleasanter subjects."

"Yes."

At dusk the beach was not crowded. A few other couples were also enjoying the beach's beauty, and some distant children ran and splashed in the shallow water. It was nearing high tide, and the beach was far narrower than it had been when Elizabeth had bathed there.

They walked east for a while, with the setting sun at their backs, watching as the waning light cast the clouds into vivid hues of gold, orange, and pink. The rhythmic sound of the waves was relaxing, and some of the tension from the past few days drained from her body. It was somehow easier to breathe here. Elizabeth sighed in contentment; the serenity of the place soothed her soul. "At times I believe I could happily spend the rest of my life on the beach."

"I know how you feel," Mr. Darcy replied. "Although I would miss trees and woods and Pemberley."

They strolled in a companionable silence. Accustomed to walking with her rather voluble sisters, Elizabeth found the quiet to be both strange and oddly comforting. The only Bennet sister who did not maintain a constant stream of chatter was Jane, but when she said something it was worth hearing. Elizabeth might say the same of Mr. Darcy. This brought a smile to her face. Who would believe those two people would have anything in common?

After several minutes of silence, Mr. Darcy cleared his throat. "I suppose they will arrest Wickham tonight."

"They may have already."

"What will you do then?"

Elizabeth stared at the horizon. "I would like to return to Hertfordshire. There is no need to remain. However, it may be difficult to convince Lydia to depart immediately, and she should not remain in Brighton without me."

He fell silent again. Only then did she realize that expressing a desire to leave Brighton might be interpreted as a wish to quit his company. "But we might linger in Brighton a week or two as well," she added.

He did not respond. *Perhaps I misinterpreted his reaction.* Finally, he lifted his head and caught her eye. "Would you...perhaps consider...a visit to Pemberley?"

Elizabeth blinked rapidly. "Pemberley?"

"I would very much like to show you Derbyshire...and my home..." He swallowed. "The grounds are very fine."

"Of course. Of course, I would love to see Pemberley," she said hastily. "But I would need—"

"A chaperone," he finished for her. "Yes, yes, of course."

Another long silence followed, broken only by the crash of waves and the crunch of sand and stone beneath their feet. "My aunt is from that part of the country," Elizabeth said finally. "She might accompany me on a visit."

"That would be…I would love to have her visit…and you, of course."

How ridiculous. We kissed on my bed. More than once. How silly that we are now so awkward and hesitant with each other. We did better when I disliked him. Perhaps he prefers frankness?

She stopped walking and faced him. "Why, Mr. Darcy," she adopted a pert tone, "are you hoping that a visit to Pemberley will convince me to accept an offer of marriage?"

A smile curled up one side of his mouth. "I do not believe an offer of marriage is on the table, madam."

She almost laughed aloud. "So you climbed into my bedchamber because…?"

"I had to warn you about Wickham. I had no other purpose in mind." He clearly repressed a smile.

"And when you kissed me?"

"Kissed you?" he exclaimed in mock horror. "I recall no kisses. Perhaps I fell against you and our lips brushed against each other, but kisses? No."

Elizabeth could maintain the charade no longer; she burst into laughter. Mr. Darcy joined her, but when their chuckles subsided, his expression was sober. "In truth, I have long been hoping to change your mind on the subject of marriage—whether it is with kisses or houses."

"Quite a devious plan, sir." He smiled at her raillery. "But I must warn you that neither kisses nor houses will tempt me." His face fell. "However, your *words* may very well accomplish that goal. I must confess to a weakness for lively conversation."

His eyes lit up. "Hmm…I will do my best to provide it."

"You have done an admirable job to this point."

He was standing quite close and spoke softly. "However, Miss Bennet, I find I have a dilemma. You enjoy my conversation, but I have a strong inclination at this moment for an activity that does not include words."

At these words Elizabeth's entire body came alive—no part of her had forgotten the marvelous kisses in her bedchamber. Her lips were greedy, and her arms were empty. She wanted more. More kisses. More caresses. More Mr. Darcy.

In the next moment Elizabeth was falling. Falling into Mr. Darcy's arms. Falling against his body. Warm lips covered hers, and a tongue pushed into her mouth, exploring and stroking. In a distant part of her mind, she knew they should not kiss in plain view of any passersby, but it was impossible to deny herself such bliss. Every second she promised herself she would stop, and every second she could not endure the thought of such deprivation.

Finally, the need for air became too acute, and she pulled away, resting her head against the front of his waistcoat. "You have an unfair advantage, sir," she mumbled.

"Hmm?" His voice was laced with amusement.

"Your kisses are nearly as persuasive as your words."

He kissed the top of her head affectionately. "I must use every advantage I have." He hugged her tightly against his chest. "Oh, Elizabeth, I pray you will come to Pemberley."

Craning her neck upward, she saw naked hope in his eyes. "I will come, Mr. Darcy. I will find a way."

She had not known he was capable of such a broad smile. "After such a kiss, perhaps you might call me William, my dear?"

"William." The syllables were awkward in her mouth, but continuing to address him as Mr. Darcy felt wrong as well.

This won her another smile. After a long pause, Mr. Dar—William peered at the darkening sky. "Perhaps we should return to the colonel's house."

"I am eager to hear how they fared with Wickham."

"Yes."

They returned the way they had come, although it was growing more difficult to see the beach clearly. The sun was hovering at the edge of the horizon but had not yet set. Elizabeth pointed to something she had noticed earlier, a wooden structure jutting out into the ocean. "What is that?"

"It is an old pier," William responded. "I believe people occasionally bring boats here during high tide or use it for fishing."

As the light diminished, a fog rolled in off the sea, and the end of the pier was cloaked in mist. Elizabeth squinted to see more clearly. "I believe there is a boat moored there now. At the very end."

"It appears so. I wonder who would venture out in a fog like this." He shrugged and steered them toward the cross street that would return them to St. James Street.

They had nearly reached the street when three figures rounded the corner ahead of them. Mr. Wickham, Mr. Harrison…and Lydia!

Elizabeth recoiled instinctively, taking several steps away from two men she knew to be very dangerous. *What are they about here? They should be at the cave!* "Lydia, why are you here?" she asked when she had regained the use of her voice.

Her sister gave Elizabeth a smug smile. "La! The house was so boring, so I went to St. James Street, where I found Wicky and his friend. They invited me for a boat ride."

Elizabeth's stomach churned. *That is their boat at the pier— waiting to take them across the Channel. They never intended to leave from the cave. Colonel Forster and his men wait in the wrong place.*

And these miscreants want to take Lydia with them?

"You cannot!" Elizabeth immediately blurted out. All three regarded her warily. *I must conceal my agitation or risk rousing their suspicions. If they discover that their secrets are known and that capture is imminent, they will be far more dangerous.* She could see that both men were armed with pistols. "Er, it is far too foggy to go out on a boat tonight," she continued in a calmer tone.

Lydia clapped her hands together. "That is part of the fun! Darkness and fog and lantern light… It will be like a pirate ship!" *More than you know*, Elizabeth thought. "You're just jealous that Wicky didn't ask you!" Lydia sneered.

"Darcy, why are you out here?" Mr. Wickham regarded the other man suspiciously.

William must have reached the same conclusion as Elizabeth, for he answered in a mild voice. "Miss Elizabeth and I were taking a stroll on the beach." The calm was belied by the coiled tension she could sense beneath her hand.

They could take Lydia to France with them—or drop her in the Channel. I must separate her from them. But how?

Instinctively she knew that the appearance of loyalty to Mr. Wickham would convey an advantage. She dropped her hand from William's arm and took a step away. "He wishes me to give you up," she told Mr. Wickham with a sneer. "It is forever his aim. He is so jealous of you."

William's head whipped around to stare at her, but she kept her gaze fixed on Mr. Wickham. *I pray that William guesses I am playacting.*

Mr. Wickham smirked. "It was ever so—even from childhood. Poor Darcy! Nobody likes you!"

If she had plunged a knife between his ribs, William could not have appeared more wounded. "Elizabeth…" The desperation in his voice nearly caused her to abandon the charade.

"We must go before the tide turns!" Mr. Harrison said fretfully to Mr. Wickham.

"Yes," his friend agreed. "A good evening to you, Darcy, Miss Elizabeth." He nodded pleasantly as if they had encountered each other at the market square. *I must prevent them from taking Lydia.* Elizabeth would never forgive herself if her sister came to harm.

Could she simply grab her sister and run? No, the men had pistols, and Lydia would not come willingly. "Take me with you!" she blurted out.

"No!" William's voice was a horrified croak.

"I would dearly love a boat ride." Elizabeth gave Mr. Wickham a coy smile, pleased to see his eyes lingering on her face.

Lydia hurried to take the officer's arm. "No! This is *my* treat!"

Mr. Wickham smiled lazily, enjoying the spectacle of two women fighting over him, but Mr. Harrison yanked on his sleeve. "We have no time for your *affaires de coeur*! We must push off now!"

"We cannot leave yet." Mr. Wickham frowned. "You know that. We must wait for—"

Mr. Harrison made a quelling motion before the other man said the name. *Ah, Colonel Forster was right; at least one other person is involved in their schemes. Blast!* Elizabeth was not eager to face yet another thug.

William chose that moment to lunge forward, grabbing Lydia's hand and trying to pull her toward him. But she clung to Mr. Wickham, who quickly pulled the pistol from his belt and brandished it at William. "Release her now."

The master of Pemberley hesitated. Elizabeth imagined what she would say if she were truly under Mr. Wickham's spell. "George, don't hurt him. You'll hang for sure! Think of your career."

With an evil grin, the officer instead pointed the pistol at Lydia's head. "Release her." William let go of her hand instantly and stepped away.

Lydia glanced sidelong at the pistol, laughing nervously. "Wicky, what are you about? Now isn't the time for your silly jokes!"

Mr. Wickham ignored her.

"I will not interfere with your departure, Wickham. Just give me Lydia," Mr. Darcy said in a level tone. Elizabeth's heart swelled, knowing he cared about Lydia for her sake.

The other man barked a laugh. "Interfere?" Mr. Harrison had produced a pistol in each hand and pointed one at Darcy. "And how, pray tell, would you manage to interfere?"

Elizabeth surveyed the surrounding beach, seeking help, but it was deserted. Soon the rolling fog would conceal them from the rest of the world.

With a hand clamped on Lydia's upper arm, Mr. Wickham dragged her backward across the sand and stone toward the pier. "Wicky," Lydia whined, "you're hurting me!"

He shook Lydia so hard that her head wobbled. "Quiet!" She was momentarily too stunned to speak.

I must find a way to free Lydia. But while Elizabeth's heart beat double time, her mind seemed to have shut down completely, unable to focus on anything except dread.

"Colonel Forster and his men are searching for you," William warned. "You will never reach France."

"France!" Lydia shrieked. "We're not going to France!" She glared at Mr. Wickham, who said nothing. "Are we going to France? Will you buy me a silk shawl? I've always wanted a silk shawl."

Mr. Wickham laughed at Darcy. "I don't see any militia."

"They are on their way," the other man promised.

The officer smirked. "Then I suppose we should leave immediately."

Mr. Harrison frowned. "What about—"

"If our colleague doesn't arrive in France with us, then we only need to split the reward two ways." Mr. Wickham's grin was oily.

"Ah," said Mr. Harrison. "Perhaps we *should* hasten our departure."

They had reached the pier. Mr. Wickham dragged Lydia onto the weather-beaten boards, walking backward so he could keep an eye on William. He and Elizabeth followed at a safe distance. "La! What fun!" Lydia trilled. "But my visit to France must be short, or Papa will be very angry with me."

The slow, awkward procession continued until they reached the end of the pier. Fog enveloped the area, cutting off the pier from the rest of the world and even muffling sound. The only noises were the creaking of the wood in the small rowing boat and the slap of water against the pier's pilings.

Elizabeth could not imagine trying to cross the Channel in such a small boat, but perhaps they planned to rendezvous with a larger French vessel.

Still threatening Lydia, Mr. Wickham waited warily as his friend hauled on the boat's moorings, pulling it up to the pier so he could clamber aboard. Elizabeth waited until Mr. Wickham had gestured for Lydia to climb aboard before she shouted. "Wait! Take me instead!"

"Elizabeth!" Darcy's voice was a horrified rasp.

She ignored him, slowly closing in on the end of the pier—step by step—holding her hands away from her body to show that she was not a threat. All her attention was focused on Mr. Wickham; success depended on convincing him of her sincere attraction to him. "Take me with you. I have no desire to remain here without you!"

He hesitated, considering, but Mr. Harrison, standing in the boat, rolled his eyes. "Damnation, Wickham, we can't take two women with us!"

"Elizabeth, no!" The agony in Darcy's voice seared itself into Elizabeth's heart, but she did not dare to glance in his direction.

"If I stay here, my parents will force me to marry Darcy," Elizabeth said. *I pray to God that William understands this is a ploy.*

"Darcy wouldn't marry you!" Wickham scoffed.

"Oh? He has already offered once, and I refused. I know he will propose again."

Mr. Wickham turned a dumbfounded expression on William. "You offered marriage to her?"

"She tells the truth," he said in a miserable voice.

"Lizzy, you sly thing!" Lydia said. "You never breathed a word."

Ignoring everyone else, Elizabeth concentrated on convincing Mr. Wickham. "Lydia will be a far more troublesome creature than I would. You know that, George."

Lydia stamped her foot. "That's not true!"

"We have no time for this! We must depart," Mr. Harrison yelled from the rocking boat.

The officer shrugged at his compatriot rather apologetically. "Elizabeth makes a good point."

"Et tu, Wicky?" Lydia protested.

Elizabeth leaned forward, giving him an enticing peek at her cleavage. "And…I speak French," she said as seductively as she could manage. "I have always *longed* to visit France."

"She's right," Mr. Wickham tossed over his shoulder at his friend. "She would be less trouble than this one."

"Fine. Pick one of them. I don't care which. I want to be gone before your 'friend' arrives!" the other man urged.

"Not *my* friend," Wickham grumbled.

"Lydia has a tendency toward seasickness," Elizabeth said quickly. "Do you want her casting up her accounts in the middle of the Channel?"

"Oh, Good Lord." Mr. Wickham rolled his eyes, and even Mr. Harrison paled at this news.

"I do not!" Lydia protested. "Well, not most of the time."

"Very well," Wickham growled at Elizabeth. "Come here." He gestured her toward him with the gun.

Just as Elizabeth was nearing the rowing boat, William made his move. Launching himself forward, he tried to tackle Wickham around the knees, but the officer was prepared for such a maneuver and swung Lydia bodily toward her would-be rescuer.

She smacked into William's chest, and his arms flew around her in a parody of a lovers' embrace as they fell together onto the rough wood of the pier. Meanwhile, Wickham grabbed Elizabeth and pulled her onto the swaying boat.

Lydia squawked and cried, "Mr. Darcy, I cannot breathe!" as William muttered, "I beg your pardon, Miss Lydia."

Ignoring the distress of two people she loved was difficult, but Elizabeth resolutely seated herself in the prow of the boat. By the time she peeked up again, Lydia and William had disentangled themselves, and the rowing boat had pushed away from the pier. As Mr. Wickham and Mr. Harrison were rowing in earnest, it was falling behind them at a rapid pace.

"No! Elizabethhhh!"

Elizabeth winced. She had never heard such desolation in William's voice; in fact, she would not have believed him capable of making such a sound.

William continued to shout as the pier receded from sight, but the sound of his words grew fainter and fainter as they were absorbed by the swirling fog—until she could no longer hear him.

Chapter Fourteen

Darcy thought he knew despair when Elizabeth had refused him at Hunsford, but that could not compare to the agony of watching a boat bearing his beloved disappear into the fog. He had believed he could thwart Wickham's plan at the last minute, but the other man had been too clever. Throwing Lydia at Darcy had delayed him just long enough to allow their escape. By the time Darcy had disentangled himself, the boat was yards from the pier.

Already the vessel was scarcely visible in the thick fog. For a wild moment he considered diving into the water, but his swimming abilities were no more than adequate—certainly not fast enough to race a boat. Instead, he was reduced to shouting threats and imprecations after Wickham.

If only he could find help! But if there were any other people on the beach, the fog concealed them thoroughly. Blast and damnation! The men most capable of rendering assistance now huddled uselessly outside a cave to the east. *I should go and find them.* But his feet refused to move. Irrationally, he could not abandon the last place he had seen Elizabeth— although there was no reason to believe the boat would return.

His mind tried to seize on slivers of hope, but he knew in his heart that they were false. Even if Wickham remained convinced that Elizabeth's passion for him was authentic, he was unlikely to return the loyalty. More likely she would outlive her usefulness once they left the pier, and Harrison would toss her overboard—while Wickham offered no objections. Simply imagining the scene made Darcy's entire body shake with impotent rage.

The best he could hope for was that Elizabeth would survive the journey across the Channel to become a prisoner in France—where she would be friendless and vulnerable. *Perhaps a quick death in the sea would be preferable.* The pain in Darcy's chest grew so fierce that he seriously considered the question of whether he was dying.

I will never see her again. I must accept the truth.

Damn Wickham for being a treacherous scoundrel!

Darcy wanted to blame Elizabeth as well, but he could not; she had sacrificed herself for her sister. Although Darcy hated the choice she had made, he was not surprised; it was entirely in keeping with her character. *Why could I not love a more selfish woman?*

Staring into the gray expanse of fog hovering over the sea, Darcy made a vow. He would devote the rest of his life to hunting down Wickham and forcing him to pay for his crimes.

After several minutes of futilely seeking any sign of the rowing boat, he turned his attention back to the pier. Despite Lydia's unworthiness, Elizabeth had ensured her sister would live, and he had an obligation to protect her.

The girl huddled on the pier's rough wooden planks, alternately bemoaning a tear in her best muslin dress and complaining about bruises on her arm. From the volume of her laments, an observer might believe she was the one whose life was currently threatened. *This is who Elizabeth sacrificed her life for!* What a pathetic exchange. Darcy was quite tempted to leave the girl to find her own way home.

Swallowing his bitterness, Darcy offered Lydia a hand and pulled her to her feet. "Miss Lydia, we should seek some help."

She examined her torn dress. "Yes, a good seamstress might repair it."

Darcy ground his teeth. "I meant we should locate someone with a boat who can pursue your sister and Wickham."

Lydia rolled her eyes. "Why? She'll return in a few days. And she'll be the one who gets a silk shawl!"

Does she even understand that we are at war with France? Darcy opened his mouth to reply but closed it again when he heard unexpected sounds: feet pounding on the other end of the pier. Someone was running in their direction. Was this Wickham's mysterious "friend"? Not for the first time Darcy wished he had brought his pistols. Placing Lydia behind him, he readied himself to fight in her defense.

However, the shape that emerged from the fog was…Mrs. Forster. Red-faced, with wisps of hair lashing her skin, the woman raced toward the end of the pier, her skirts hitched up around her knees. Ignoring the others, she stopped at the end of the pier, searching the water with wild eyes.

At the sight of her friend, Lydia grinned and clapped her hands. "Mary! You cannot imagine what has occurred! Wickham was here with another man and—"

Mrs. Forster made a visible effort to calm herself, smoothing her hair and turning to Lydia with a wan attempt at a smile. "What is this? Wickham, you say, and another man? Where are they at this minute?"

Lydia babbled a garbled account of all that had transpired, but Darcy did not attend to it. Instead, he observed Mrs. Forster warily. Her appearance at this moment was entirely too coincidental, and she was far too concerned with Wickham's whereabouts. When Lydia finished her tale, Mrs. Forster gave a rather forced laugh, placing a hand delicately over her mouth. "Such goings on! I cannot imagine what Mr. Wickham was about."

Various puzzle pieces fell into place. "You are Wickham's friend!" Darcy cried. "The one he and Harrison left behind." Blast it all! Forster's own wife had been spying on him. No wonder the French had learned so many secret plans.

Mrs. Forster regarded him with wide and wounded eyes. "I do not know what you mean."

Darcy shook his head in disgust. "Of course, Forster never discovered who was ferreting out his regiment's secret plans." As Richard said, nobody ever suspected women of espionage.

The woman gave a little laugh. "I believe you are confused..."

He stepped forward until his tall form loomed over her smaller frame. "*They* may have escaped justice, but I will see that *you* are turned over to the magistrate."

Instantly, the innocent young woman disappeared as a cold and calculated expression swept over her face. In a deft move, she produced a pistol from her reticule and pointed it at Darcy with a steadiness that suggested she knew how to use it. He froze. *How often can I be threatened with pistols in one day?*

"You have a pistol, too?" Lydia wailed. "Everyone has a pistol except me!"

"The boat is departed," Darcy said to Mrs. Forster. "You cannot escape now."

"How unfortunate for you," she sneered. "Since I am condemned to this benighted island, it is imperative that nobody reveal my true identity." *She would kill me and Lydia without any compunction.*

Mrs. Forster gestured for Darcy to raise his hands, and he obliged, silently fuming at himself that he had not previously identified her as the traitor. If the realization had arrived even seconds earlier, he might have captured her.

She shook her head in a parody of sympathy. "What a waste. Mr. Darcy, such a handsome man. So unfortunate that he was shot by smugglers in Brighton."

"There are smugglers?" Lydia gasped, looking about with wide eyes.

Mrs. Forster smirked at Darcy. "She is so delightfully dull it is almost a shame I must shoot her as well. But there is a chance—well, a remote chance—she might accurately report on today's events."

"Who are you shooting, Mary?" Lydia asked.

The other woman gestured to Lydia with the pistol. "Go and stand beside him." As Lydia edged closer to Darcy, he could not help noticing that they were conveniently positioned at the very end of the pier, where their bodies would simply fall into the water. *Well, I will not have long to mourn Elizabeth.*

But he did not want this evil woman to triumph. Desperately, Darcy thought about any way he could distract or delay her. "Are you the one who killed Mr. Denny?" he asked.

A brief expression of regret passed over her face. "When he discovered my 'activities,' I offered him the opportunity to join our band and make his fortune, but the fool declined. Wickham was supposed to do the deed, but he grew too squeamish at the last minute." Darcy found it less than reassuring to know she had murdered one man already.

Lydia gasped audibly, finally comprehending the gravity of their circumstances. "You can't shoot me, Mary! I'm your friend. I lent you my bonnet!"

Ignoring the other woman, Mrs. Forster shook her head, and her expression turned steely. "Enough talk. I should take my leave." She aimed the pistol right at Darcy's heart.

***

With Harrison and Wickham rowing rapidly, the boat quickly pulled away from the pier, which was soon lost to sight. As the sound of William's voice was swallowed by the fog, Elizabeth tried not to imagine the agony he was experiencing. Instead, she focused on implementing her plan, thankful that the two men had their backs to her.

Fortunately, she had worn a front-lacing dress, so she could untie her own laces and draw the overdress over her head, leaving her in the shift underneath. Keeping her feet tucked under the hem of the skirt, she then unbuckled and removed her half boots. The bonnet was one of her favorites, and she laid it on the bottom of the boat with a pang of regret.

Now she was ready. She gathered her feet underneath her, preparing to jump before the boat was too far from the pier. Once she was in the water, the two men were unlikely to waste time searching for her, assuming she would drown. Elizabeth just prayed that assumption would be wrong. She had never swum such a long distance.

Just as she was about to plunge off the side of the boat, Mr. Wickham turned and noticed her. "What the hell? Damnation, woman—!" He reached out—rather unwisely in Elizabeth's opinion—with an oar in a vain attempt to keep her seated in the prow. At the sound of Wickham's voice, Harrison whirled around, smacking his oar into the other man's jaw.

Elizabeth did not hesitate. She jumped only seconds before the momentum of the blow propelled Wickham into the water. The impact of two bodies falling over the same side of the boat immediately caused it to capsize.

Get away! Get away! Get away! Elizabeth swam as fast as she could under the water, putting as much distance between herself and the boat as possible.

She surfaced only when her lungs were screaming for air. Already she was far enough away that the boat was a dim shape in the fog. The silhouette told her it was upside down in the water while two dark figures clung to it, yelling profanities. Elizabeth was relieved that neither man had drowned.

"I cannot swim! I cannot swim!" Harrison cried out again and again.

"And you suppose I can?" Wickham shouted.

The frantic sounds of splashing were followed by Wickham's voice. "Where is she? Where's the hellcat? I will shoot her the instant I see her!" In the dim light his head moved back and forth, scanning the water, although he never looked in the right direction.

"You idiot!" Harrison screamed. "Wet gunpowder won't work. Help me right the boat!"

Elizabeth did not wait to hear more. It was sufficient to know that they would not pursue her. She turned toward the faint pinpricks of lantern light that led her to Brighton. It seemed dreadfully far. Farther than she had ever swum before.

William is waiting for me. Taking a deep breath and saying a prayer, she started to swim.

***

At this range, there was no way Mrs. Forster's bullet could possibly miss striking Darcy. Her finger curved around the trigger. Watching the tiniest movements of her hand, Darcy prepared himself to jump. If he launched himself at Lydia at just the right moment, he could knock them both off the pier and into the water before the gun fired. At least that was his hope. Once they were in the water, the dim light and fog would prevent Mrs. Forster from finding and shooting them. It was a feeble plan, Darcy knew, but he refused to surrender to despair.

However, before the woman could pull the trigger, footsteps thundered at the far end of the pier. The fog concealed the identities of the newcomers, but a voice called out of the mist. "Ahoy! Darcy, are you there? Maria thought she glimpsed you. I brought her for a walk on the beach!"

Darcy cursed his bad fortune. There were many people he would have been pleased to see at that moment, primarily Richard or one of Forster's soldiers. The prince regent was not high on that list—not on the list at all, in fact. Darcy had already sent the woman he loved to her death. Would he now be responsible for the demise of a royal prince?

The prince waddled precariously into view, causing every board on the pier to groan under his weight. Mrs. Fitzherbert held his arm, propping him into an upright position, but there was no sign of his guards. Why had the prince left them behind now?

"I even slipped away from my guards for a bit. Ahoy, Darcy and Miss...Benson!" he called to them, the picture of good cheer.

"Bennet!" Lydia corrected loudly.

"Oh yes, Bennet; forgive me!" The prince giggled as if he found his own mistake amusing.

As the man lumbered toward them, Darcy sought the words that could alert the prince to the danger—without encouraging Mrs. Forster to consider him a target.

A cleverer man might have noticed the tension in the air—or the gun in Mrs. Forster's hand—but the prince was oblivious. "What, ho? You have *two* ladies now!" the prince exclaimed. "You are a sly one, Darcy!"

Mrs. Forster's eyes were wide with shock. "Is that...?"

"No," Darcy said quickly.

"La! It's the prince regent!" Lydia squealed. "Now I've seen the prince regent! Maria Lucas will be so jealous." She took a few steps toward the prince. "Would you please, please invite me to your next ball? I could wear my new green silk gown!"

The prince frowned at Lydia. "Was Miss Bennet not shorter? Is this a different one?"

Darcy did not bother to reply; he could not allow his attention to waver from Mrs. Forster's pistol—which was now aimed at the prince. A nasty smile thinned her lips. "His death would be worth a lot to Napoleon…"

Darcy's heart pounded against his ribs; this was precisely the realization he had hoped she would not have. "Mrs. Forster, do not be foolish," he warned her. "All of England would be out for your blood. You would never escape the country."

She had backed into the far corner of the pier; from there she could shoot either the prince or Darcy. "But I would be handsomely rewarded in France." Her eyes narrowed as she trained the pistol on the prince, who was nearly within range.

"Your Highness," Darcy yelled, "come no farther! She wants to shoot you!"

The prince squinted at Lydia. "But she doesn't have a pistol—" His eyes swung over to Mrs. Forster. "Oh!" He drew himself up to his full height, which was not terribly impressive, and glowered at the woman. "Miss, it is a hanging offense to threaten a member of the royal family with a firearm. Cease at once!"

Mrs. Forster laughed rather maniacally but made no move to drop the weapon. Hoping to take advantage of her momentary distraction, Darcy edged closer to her location, but she immediately targeted him with the pistol. "Come no closer! I will shoot."

Damnation! How could Darcy protect the prince, not to mention Mrs. Fitzherbert and Lydia? Success would require tackling her at precisely the right moment—and there was a high likelihood Darcy would be shot. But there was nothing for it; he would not have the prince regent's death on his conscience.

Mrs. Forster was taking aim at the prince—her attention all too focused. Knowing he had only seconds to act, Darcy prepared to leap at her. If only her concentration could be momentarily disrupted—

Without warning, a sea monster erupted out of the water and onto the opposite corner of the pier. Dripping water and trailing a few pieces of seaweed, it grabbed the edge of the pier and pulled itself onto the weathered boards. Gaping in shock, Mrs. Forster swung the pistol in the monster's direction. Seizing his opportunity, Darcy launched himself at her, knocking her off her feet and onto the wooden planks. The pistol discharged, but the bullet fired harmlessly into the air.

Finally grasping the danger, the prince regent fell to the wood of the pier and pulled his mistress on top of him.

Mrs. Forster struggled to escape, but Darcy kept her pinned to the pier with the weight of his body, trying not to think about how inappropriate the contact was. Unwinding his cravat, he used it to tie Mrs. Forster's hands behind her back, ignoring her protestations and curses.

Then he turned to face the sea monster—which resolved itself into the figure of a dark-haired woman wearing a wet shift. She was dripping and panting for breath; a piece of seaweed was draped over one shoulder. He had never seen a more beautiful sight. "Elizabeth!" Darcy crossed the pier in two strides and pulled her into his arms, heedless of his clothing. "Oh, Good Lord! I thought I had lost you forever."

Placing his hands on both sides of her head, he drew her in for a deep kiss. She kissed him back with abandon, only to pull away from him a few seconds later. "William, we are in public!"

"Yes, we are," he agreed and kissed her again.

She had miraculously returned to him; he was not about to allow nonsensical rules of propriety prevent him from expressing his gratitude and deep abiding love.

He did take a minute to examine her, surveying her from head to foot. Her hair fell in wet clumps about her neck and shoulders, and she shivered in the cool night air. She appeared exhausted but unharmed. "Are you well?" he asked with some urgency. "Did they hurt you?"

She shook wet hair from her face. "I am well, but I must say, Mr. Darcy, that when I suggested a walk on the beach, I did not anticipate obtaining quite so much exercise."

He chuckled.

Urgently, she grasped both his arms and held his eyes. "You are aware that my declarations of devotion to Wickham were false, are you not? I only said them to save Lydia."

A slow smile spread across his face. "I did not believe for one second that you truly preferred Wickham."

Her shoulders sagged. "Good, because my heart belongs to you." Darcy's breath caught. "I love you, William."

His heart was so full it might burst from his chest. "I love you, too."

The subsequent kiss was interrupted by the arrival of the prince regent's guard. The captain of the guard was pale and frantic after searching the beach for their charge, who seemed to suffer from no guilt or regret. Guards and servants hastily surrounded the prince, and one man took custody of Mrs. Forster. They tried to chivvy the prince back toward the town, but he insisted on lumbering over to speak with Darcy and Elizabeth. "Today you have saved the life of the prince regent!" he thundered grandly.

Elizabeth made a wet and sloppy curtsey while Darcy bowed. "It was my honor, Your Highness." He could only be relieved that the prince had not chosen to blame them for placing him in danger in the first place.

"You shall be rewarded!" the prince said with great solemnity. After a pause to consider, he nodded. "Yes, I will have *both* of you to dine at the Royal Pavilion! Darcy, write to my secretary to secure the engagement."

"I will, Your Highness," Darcy replied, reminding himself that excessive royal approbation was better than royal condemnation. The prince inclined his head with the air of a man bestowing a great favor and then allowed himself to be escorted back toward the town.

Despite the warmth of the evening, Elizabeth was shivering in her wet clothing. The shift clung to her curves rather becomingly, but Darcy preferred not to share that view with others. Pulling off his jacket, he placed it around Elizabeth's shoulders, unconcerned if sea water ruined the fine fabric. The garment hung off Elizabeth's slender frame, but it covered her to her knees.

Darcy was particularly pleased with this precaution when Richard arrived with a group of soldiers a few minutes later. After returning from their fruitless wait at the cave, the two colonels had encountered the prince and his guards. Colonel Forster had accompanied the royal guards to the magistrate, where his wife would be jailed. Discovering his wife's treachery must have been a cruel shock to the man.

Elizabeth told Richard the story about her escape from the boat, prompting Darcy to thank providence she had survived. How easily he could have lost her! Richard dispatched a few soldiers to obtain a boat so they might search for Wickham and Harrison. Hopefully the scoundrels had not managed to right their vessel and escape to France.

For several minutes, the end of the pier was the source of much activity. Richard issued orders as soldiers raced away on various tasks. A shivering Elizabeth answered questions from many different sources while

Darcy hovered protectively. And somehow Lydia managed to get in everybody's way.

Noticing how Elizabeth was drooping with fatigue, Darcy stacked some empty crates into a makeshift bench and sat huddled beside her, trying to share his body heat while she patiently described the location and direction of Wickham's boat.

Finally, one soldier brought a blanket, which Darcy wrapped around Elizabeth. It calmed her shivers, but he was still eager to get her into a house and warmer clothing. She was determined to remain as long as she might be of assistance. Darcy grew more anxious as the lines of fatigue around her mouth deepened.

Colonel Forster arrived to take command of the situation, shooting Darcy more than one disapproving glare. *I suppose I am sitting rather close to her—and my arm* is *around her shoulders.* He did not remember placing it there. *Perhaps I earned the glare.* But Darcy refused to move away from her.

Maybe he should have been more concerned about Elizabeth's reputation, but he was fairly confident they would shortly be betrothed—and she was perfectly capable of objecting to the placement of his hand. She did not object, and even leaned more heavily on his shoulder as fatigue caught up to her.

Darcy would have been pleased to focus all his attention on Elizabeth and forget Lydia, but the girl refused to be ignored. Despite the noise created by multiple officers shouting and tromping around the pier, Lydia's wails could be easily discerned. "Did you see that bruise? I believe my arm might be broken! And my nerves are in such a state! I must tell you—"

After several minutes of such recitations, Elizabeth summoned her sister to her side and gestured for her to sit on a nearby crate. "Did you notice my bruises, Lizzy?" the girl demanded immediately.

Elizabeth examined them with far more seriousness than they deserved, but at least Lydia had ceased wailing. "Thank providence you were not more grievously injured," Elizabeth said finally. "Or worse."

"Worse?" Lydia repeated blankly.

Elizabeth nodded solemnly. "We are blessed to have learned Mr. Wickham's evil nature now, as painful as the discovery was. It would have been ever so much worse to learn of the flaws in his character if you had eloped with him."

Lydia stuck out her chin. "I would never have eloped with him! I did not like him so very much."

Elizabeth exchanged an amused glance with Darcy but merely said, "I am happy to hear that." The following silence was broken only by Lydia's complaints about the breeze.

Apparently, the youngest Miss Bennet had been observing the soldiers over several minutes, for she finally said to Darcy, "Your cousin, Colonel Fitzwilliam, looks very well in his regimentals." Not believing a response was required, Darcy said nothing. "Is he married...or betrothed?"

This does not bode well for Richard. Briefly, Darcy considered inventing a betrothal for his cousin. "No, he is not." He felt like a traitor simply by relaying the information.

Lydia bounced up from her seat. "Perhaps I might be of some assistance to him."

Bounding toward Richard, she commenced pestering him with questions, which he answered with a bemused expression. After several minutes of Lydia's attention, Richard gave Darcy a beseeching look, but Darcy just shrugged; he was not about to leave Elizabeth's side. If his cousin could not handle a girl of fifteen years, he was not much of a soldier.

Another shiver wracked Elizabeth's body, and Darcy pulled the blanket more tightly around her. How soon will she wish to return to Longbourn? Would she want to leave tomorrow? The next day? The thought sobered him; he did not want to be separated from her for any length of time.

Elizabeth nestled against his side, fitting perfectly. "Elizabeth?" he murmured.

"Hmm?" Her smile was tired but still thoroughly enchanting.

"I very much would like to make you an offer of marriage. Would you fuss if I did so now, or would you prefer that I wait for a more appropriate moment?"

Elizabeth blinked in surprise and then gave a soft chuckle. "Are you asking for permission to propose to me?"

He shrugged. "Well, these are not the ideal circumstances, but I am loath to allow further delays. And a betrothal might forestall some of Colonel Forster's baleful glares in my direction."

After a quick peek at the scowling colonel, Elizabeth nodded. "Very well, Mr. Darcy. I give you permission to make me an offer of marriage."

If she refuses me now, I will feel like an idiot.

Taking hold of Elizabeth's hand, Darcy stood and then bent on one knee to kneel before Elizabeth's seated form. Lydia squealed, and a hush fell over the soldiers. *I had not anticipated such an audience, but oh well...*

"Miss Elizabeth Bennet," he said, his voice husky and low, "I cannot possibly express how much I admire and love you. Will you consent to be my wife?"

She did not leave him in suspense. The sweetest smile imaginable spread over her lips. "Yes, Mr. Fitzwilliam Darcy, I will marry you."

The kiss that followed was overly long—even by the generous standard for betrothed couples. If anyone objected, Darcy did not notice.

Epilogue

"My shoes are simply full of sand!"

Elizabeth shrugged at her mother's sour face. "I apologize, Mama."

"Of all the foolish ideas!" her mother exclaimed. "Whoever heard of being married at a beach!"

"Your ordeal is nearly finished," Elizabeth observed mildly. She and William had known that her mother and sundry other guests at the wedding ceremony would consider a beach venue to be peculiar—or even a personal affront—but they had loved the idea and advanced with the plans while preparing for criticism. "If you like, you may proceed to the wedding breakfast early."

Now that the ceremony was complete, Elizabeth and William were mingling and greeting their guests, which included the Earl of Matlock and other high-ranking personages. Mrs. Bennet scanned the crowd and patted her coiffure. "Not just yet, I think."

Elizabeth suppressed a smile; no doubt her mother hoped her unwed daughters might encounter other rich men at this event. As if on cue, her mother murmured in her ear, "Who is the man speaking with Kitty?"

"I believe he is a viscount's heir." No other words could have prompted Mrs. Bennet to move with such alacrity. She was standing at Kitty's side within seconds. *I hope she does not scare away the poor man.*

Any lingering frustration with her mother was instantly dispelled when William came beside Elizabeth and took her hand in his warm, firm grasp. "Was your mother generously bestowing her opinion on the wedding venue again?" he asked and then chuckled when she nodded. "Indeed, I just heard Miss Bingley's view on that subject—and realized we are fortunate Aunt Catherine did not accept the invitation."

The thought of Lady Catherine de Bourgh with sand in her shoes caused Elizabeth to shudder. "Indeed."

Holding a wedding ceremony at a beach *was* an unusual idea, but Elizabeth had loved it from the moment William had suggested it. Since the events surrounding Wickham and Harrison's attempted escape three weeks ago, the couple had taken many happy strolls along the beach;

fortunately, none were as eventful as the first one. Elizabeth believed William nearly loved the seaside as much as she did.

Once during the preparations, the doubts of friends and family caused Elizabeth to second-guess their decision, but William reminded her that they had recently faced life-or-death situations and survived. "I believe we are entitled to hold our wedding service wherever we would like," he had said with a kiss to the top of her head.

Elizabeth's mother had predicted they would never find a priest to perform the ceremony, but the prestige of the Darcy name had readily solved that dilemma—and eased the process of obtaining a special license. Much dismay had also been expressed over their brief engagement, but neither Elizabeth nor William wished to wait, and the shortened time span kept Mrs. Bennet's interference to a minimum.

Elizabeth had no regrets. The ceremony had been everything she hoped for. Bright sunshine sparkled and glinted off the water while the waves provided a soothing background noise. William's face had glowed with happiness as he had recited his wedding vows, and Elizabeth had no doubt hers mirrored it. She would cherish these memories, and the guests would soon forget the sand in their shoes.

Scanning the crowd, she realized that she and William had greeted nearly everyone there. "Perhaps it is time to go to the Pavilion?"

William squeezed her hand. "Yes. I am famished!"

Colonel Fitzwilliam arrived in time to hear this exchange. "Excellent! I was just about to warn you that your troops need sustenance. An army travels on its stomach."

"I do not believe we have an army's worth of guests." William chuckled at his cousin.

"We have quite a wedding banquet ready for them at the Pavilion," Elizabeth assured Richard.

The prince regent had not forgotten that William and Elizabeth had saved his life. When he learned they would wed in Brighton, he had offered the use of his home for their wedding breakfast. Although it was an elegant building, they had been unsure about whether to accept the offer. However, when they learned that the prince would be in London and unable to attend the event, they accepted the offer with alacrity. Elizabeth's mother had been speechless with happiness at this news; even Miss Bingley had deigned to be impressed.

"Was there news from London?" Elizabeth asked the colonel. He had been awaiting word of the verdict in the trial of Mrs. Forster, Mr. Harrison, and Mr. Wickham, which had taken place the day before.

He gave her a satisfied smile. "Yes. They were all found guilty. Although they have not yet received sentences, I am sure they will be transported at the very least."

"That would be best for Colonel Forster," Elizabeth said, glancing at the man, who was flirting rather outrageously with a few female wedding guests. He had initiated divorce proceedings and apparently was already seeking a new wife.

Colonel Fitzwilliam frowned. "Yes. The colonel is fortunate he was not cashiered from the militia, but he explained that their families arranged the marriage and he spent little time with his wife. The investigation cleared him of any complicity."

Elizabeth noticed the man smile at a young woman. "I hope he plans to spend more time with the future Mrs. Forster."

"Indeed."

William was surveying the milling crowd of guests. "Richard, could I prevail upon you to gather up the wedding guests and encourage them to walk in the direction of the Pavilion? I would imagine your leadership skills are up to the challenge."

His cousin gave a mock grimace. "Civilians are so troublesome to command."

"You may promise them good food and even better company," Elizabeth said teasingly.

"Now there are incentives the army never offers," Richard said. "Very well, I will encourage everyone to move in a purposeful direction." He gave William a mocking salute and a wink before marching toward the revelers.

We should join them, Elizabeth thought, but her gaze was caught by the view of the sea—sparkling waters and deep blue sky. A light breeze played with her hair, and the sun warmed her skin. William did not seem to be in a hurry either. Both arms around her waist, he pulled her against his body and kissed the sensitive skin below her ear.

Her face grew warm. "We are in public!" she whispered, trying and failing to sound scandalized by his actions.

He chuckled. "Everyone here knows how I feel about you, dearest." Indeed, none of the guests paid any attention as they began to drift toward the town—and the breakfast. "What would you say to a house by the sea? We could purchase one for the next summer," he murmured in her ear.

"That would be lovely! But perhaps not at Brighton. Perhaps a more isolated location."

"My thoughts precisely."

Elizabeth vibrated with excitement. "We could sail a boat, and I could teach the children to swim—both the boys and the girls."

William sucked in a breath. "How many children do you believe we will have?"

"Well, Mama had five..." Elizabeth shrugged.

"Five! I had not thought of so many."

She patted his hand where it rested on her waist. "They do not arrive all at once, my dear."

They watched the sparkling water for a long moment, then Elizabeth cleared her throat. "Richard asked me if I would be interested in working for the Home Office. Apparently, they have decided to recruit some female agents."

All of William's muscles stiffened. "How did you reply?"

"I told him it was an excellent idea, but I have no further interest in espionage. Recent events provided quite enough excitement for one lifetime." She could feel her new husband sag with relief. "I did, however, recommend that he ask Mary if she would be interested."

"Mary? Your sister?"

"Indeed. She is intelligent and good at keeping secrets."

His hands tightened around her waist. "She might make a good spy, but it cannot please your mother. She will meet few eligible men that way."

Elizabeth laughed.

After a moment, he released her waist and grabbed her hand. "Come, we should not be late to our own wedding breakfast."

Elizabeth nodded in agreement but continued to stare at the sea, reluctant to leave.

He squeezed her hand. "I promise you will visit the ocean again. I will bring you to the beach as often as you like."

Turning toward him, she threw her arms around his neck. "I am pleased to hear that, Mr. Darcy, for the beach is even more dear to me now than it was."

He smiled down at her. "Oh?"

"Yes, for it was at the seaside that I fell in love with you."

The End

Thank you for purchasing this book. I know you have many entertainment options, and I appreciate your spending your time with my story.   Support from readers like you makes it possible for independent authors like me to continue writing.

Reviews are a book's lifeblood.

Please consider leaving a review where you purchased the book.

Learn more about me and my upcoming releases:

Sign up for my newsletter *Dispatches from Pemberley*

Website: www.victoriakincaid.com

Twitter: VictoriaKincaid @kincaidvic

Blog: https://kincaidvictoria.wordpress.com/

Facebook: https://www.facebook.com/kincaidvictoria

About Victoria Kincaid

The author of numerous best-selling *Pride and Prejudice* variations, historical romance writer Victoria Kincaid has a Ph.D. in English literature and runs a small business, er, household with two children, a hyperactive dog, an overly affectionate cat, and a husband who is not threatened by Mr. Darcy. They live near Washington DC, where the inhabitants occasionally stop talking about politics long enough to complain about the traffic.

On weekdays she is a freelance writer/editor who now specializes in IT marketing (it's more interesting than it sounds). In the past, some of her more…unusual writing subjects have included space toilets, taxi services, laser gynecology, bidets, orthopedic shoes, generating energy from onions, Ferrari rental car services, and vampire face lifts (she swears she is not making any of this up). A lifelong Austen fan, Victoria has read more Jane Austen variations and sequels than she can count – and confesses to an extreme partiality for the Colin Firth version of *Pride and Prejudice*.

The Unforgettable Mr. Darcy

Mr. Darcy arrives at Longbourn, intending to correct the mistakes he made during his disastrous proposal in Hunsford. To his horror, he learns that Elizabeth Bennet was killed in a ship's explosion off the coast of France—in an apparent act of sabotage. Deep in despair, he travels in disguise to wartime France to seek out the spy responsible for her death.

But a surprise awaits Darcy in the French town of Saint-Malo: Elizabeth is alive!

Recovering from a blow to the head, Elizabeth has no memory of her previous life, and a series of mistakes lead her to believe that Darcy is her husband. However, they have even bigger problems. As they travel through a hostile country, the saboteur mobilizes Napoleon's network of spies to capture them and prevent them from returning home. Elizabeth slowly regains her memories, but they often leave her more confused.

Darcy will do anything to help Elizabeth reach England safely, but what will she think of him when she learns the truth of their relationship?

Other Books by Victoria Kincaid:

The Unforgettable Mr. Darcy

President Darcy

Darcy's Honor

The Secrets of Darcy and Elizabeth

Pride and Proposals

Mr. Darcy to the Rescue

Darcy vs. Bennet

Chaos Comes to Longbourn

Christmas at Darcy House

A Very Darcy Christmas

When Jane Got Angry

When Mary Met the Colonel

www.ingramcontent.com/pod-product-compliance
Lightning Source LLC
Chambersburg PA
CBHW022028170626
46808CB00003B/1106